1

THE DRATTED Santa suit itched.

A lot.

In fact, Sam Stevenson realized with dawning horror, the suit was infested with fleas. Vigorously, he scratched an ear. He had to get out of this blasted thing before the merciless bugs flayed his meat from the bone. He did not intend to let children sit on his lap and risk passing the torture on to them.

"I gotta go," he muttered to the slender elf standing on the podium beside their sleigh, which consisted of an elaborately painted cardboard-and-plywood structure.

"Go?" The young woman blinked at him. "What do you mean? The store opens in two minutes and a mob of kids are waiting outside to see Santa. You can't go anywhere."

If he wasn't so uncomfortable he might have taken the time to admire the way her short, ginger-ale-colored hair curled about her sweet gamin face. A face for which she had obviously been hired, but Sam could think of nothing except stripping off his britches as quickly as possible.

"Listen, lady, I've got something I have to take care of. The kids will just have to wait." Sam started for the exit.

Miss Pixie sprang forward, arms outstretched, blocking his way. The jingle bells on her red-and-white striped elf hat jangled merrily as she moved. "I'm sorry, but you're not leaving."

"Excuse me?" Sam scratched furiously at his neck. What was this woman's problem? He was certain the department store wasn't paying her enough to act as his warden. "Are you telling me what I can and cannot do?"

"I know what's going on here, and I want to tell you that I don't approve." She sank her hands on her hips and frowned. Stern condemnation glistened in her olive green eyes.

Sudden apprehension rumbled through Sam. Could she have somehow guessed his secret?

"What are you talking about?" Sam clawed at his beard. The buggers were eating him alive. He had to get out of this vermin-plagued costume. Now.

"I know what's going on and I can help. My mother is a social worker."

"I don't care if your mother is Margaret Mead, get outta my way."

"Margaret Mead was an anthropologist," she corrected. "Not a sociologist. An anthropologist studies mankind. A sociologist studies social groups."

"Who gives a rat's patoot?"

"Anger." She shook her head. "A classic symptom."

Openmouthed, Sam paused long enough to stare at her. The woman was certifiable.

He tried to sidestep around her but she anticipated his move and went with him step for step as if they were waltzing.

"It's nothing to be ashamed of," she continued earnestly.

Okay, maybe having fleas was nothing to be ashamed of but Sam didn't wish to announce his plight to the entire world. In that moment he remembered a particularly humiliating experience that had happened to him in fourth grade when his favorite teacher, Miss Applebee, had discovered lice in his hair.

Sam cringed at the uncomfortable memory. The suit had to come off. Not only because of the fleas, which were indeed reason enough, but because the besieged costume reminded him of his poverty-stricken childhood.

He raised a finger and wagged it under her nose. "Get out of my way, sweetheart, or I swear I'll walk over you."

"The children are depending on you. You represent something pure and honest and wonderful. How can you shatter their dreams? Don't those little kids mean more to you than alcohol?"

"Alcohol?"

"I know a lot of the store Santas who've been hired this season are down on their luck. Men who can't hold regular jobs because they have drug and alcohol problems. Men who just need a helping hand and someone to care about them. It's not your fault that you're an addict but it *is* your responsibility to stop drinking."

Sam threw his hands in the air. "You're a lunatic, you know that? I'm not an alcoholic."

"Denial!" she crowed triumphantly. "Another classic symptom."

Swiveling his head, Sam searched for redemption from this verdant-eyed zealot, and got none.

Instead, the sight of at least three-dozen shoppers and their ardent offspring bearing down on him at warp speed assaulted his eyes.

"Santa. Santa," the children chanted.

Yikes! He had to escape. Sam faked left, then went right and sprinted past the pixie.

"Hey," she cried, "you can't expect me to face these excited kids alone. They want Santa."

People in hell want ice water. The phrase ran through his head, but he didn't say it.

The elf woman chased after him and grabbed the tail of his Santa jacket before he could bolt through the door marked Employees Only.

"You're not going anywhere, Santa," she growled out and dug in her heels. "And if you do, I'll report you to the store manager, Mr. Trotter."

Sam bared his teeth and willed the fleas to jump onto her. He tried to shake her off, but she held on with more tenacity than carpet lint on a wool jacket.

''Look, Mommy, that elf is trying to hurt Santa,'' a childish voice said.

Oh great. Now they had an audience.

''Let go,'' Sam demanded through gritted teeth.

''No.'' She narrowed her eyes and clung tighter.

Sam grabbed the corner of his jacket and jerked hard, intending on dislodging her. Instead, he ended up dragging her closer to him.

He saw a dusting of freckles across the bridge of her cute little nose, a tiny half-moon scar on her otherwise flawless forehead. Another time, another place and he would have admired her tenacity. But not here, not now, not with fleas feasting on his flesh.

''Mommy, Mommy, make that elf leave Santa alone!''

''You're scaring my daughter,'' a woman in the crowd protested.

This wasn't right. He shouldn't be drawing attention to himself. The whole point of this stakeout was to hide behind Santa's jovial facade. His boss, Chief Timmons, would have Sam's hide if he blew his cover on the very first day.

Sam had known this was going to be an awful assignment. Chief Timmons made it clear that this stint as Santa was punishment for blowing up the mayor's brand-new Lexus during his last undercover duty, never mind that it had been an unavoidable accident.

The fleas were gnawing as if they hadn't had a meal since last Christmas. Sam couldn't help wondering if Carmichael's, the famed Dallas department store, had stowed the mangy suit at a dog kennel. He couldn't take any more of this. Something had to be done.

Sam clamped his hand over the pixie's wrist and pried her fingers loose. Then, before she had time to get another hold, he bolted through the door.

Once in the vacant storeroom, he ripped the beard off and scraped his face with the vigor of a poodle scratching at full throttle. Next, he snatched the bedraggled felt hat from his head and flung it to the floor.

His fingers grappled with the big black buttons on the front of his suit, fleas hopping in all directions. He jerked off the padding strapped around his waist to simulate Santa's bulk, kicked off his boots and shucked down his pants, his mind on one thing only.

Relief.

What he hadn't counted on was that relentless, do-gooding female elf with the persistence of an Attica prison guard.

She burst through the door, catching him standing there in nothing but his briefs.

SHE'D CAUGHT Santa with his pants down.

Edie Preston came to a screeching halt. Her mouth

She'd caught Santa with his trousers down!

Edie Preston came to a screeching halt. Her mouth dropped. She had no idea that Santa was so muscular, so manly, so sexy. And she certainly didn't expect to find him almost naked in the storeroom.

Sam snapped his head around and deep sapphire eyes sliced into hers, forcing Edie's gaze to the floor.

"What is it?" Sam's voice cut like slivered glass.

"I—I—" All Edie could think of was that she'd promised to keep her hands off sexy Santa Sam...

Dear Reader

What better way to spend a day than making people laugh? My father, who writes comedy songs, taught me this at an early age. My endearingly goofy husband, who creates the most hysterical answering machine messages you'll ever hear, reinforced this lesson too.

My father was forever telling jokes and singing silly ditties. I grew up thinking all dads went around the house wearing a chicken hat and blacking out their teeth just to make their kids laugh.

I suppose it was little wonder that on our first blind date four years ago my future husband won my heart when he met me at the zoo wearing a pair of huge rainbow-coloured sunglasses and warning me not to mistake him for a baboon.

These two wonderful men have given me so much joy and love over the years that I felt compelled to write a romantic comedy to honour them.

I hope you love reading *Santa's Sexy Secret* as much as I loved writing it. I'm so thrilled to be able to share with you this story of a reluctant Santa and the heartwarming elf who teaches him what love and laughter are all about.

Happy holidays!

Lori Wilde

SANTA'S SEXY SECRET

BY
LORI WILDE

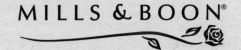

MILLS & BOON®

To my father, owner and CEO of Windmill Music,
who taught me everything he knows about writing,
and to his own creation, Tin Panny Lou.
Daddy, I love you.

*First published in Great Britain 2002
Harlequin Mills & Boon Limited,
Eton House, 18-24 Paradise Road, Richmond, Surrey TW9 1SR*

© Laurie Vanzura 2000

ISBN 0 263 83051 9

*Set in Times Roman 10½ on 12 pt.
02-1202-35542*

*Printed and bound in Spain
by Litografia Rosés, S.A., Barcelona*

dropped. She had no idea that Santa was so muscular, so manly, so gosh-darned sexy. And she certainly hadn't expected to find him almost naked in the storeroom.

What she had expected was some flabby, middle-aged drunk sucking whiskey from a flask or popping a handful of pills, not a young, vital hunk-among-hunks in a very compromising position.

He snapped his head around and deep sapphire eyes sliced into hers forcing Edie's gaze to the floor.

"What is it?" His voice cut like slivered glass. "What do you want from me?"

"I—I—" Her gaze hitched a ride from his sturdy ankles to his hard firm buttocks. Her face heated hotter than a curling iron on the highest setting. She could not seem to find her tongue even though she was sure it lay in its usual place on the floor of her mouth.

"If you've gotten your eyes full could you leave me in peace?" He turned toward her.

"I—er—didn't mean…" she stammered, unable to wrench her gaze from the spectacular sight of Santa's washboard abs.

What was a man like this doing playing Santa at a mall department store? He should be modeling underwear or playing professional sports.

"What am I supposed to do about those children?" She gestured helplessly toward the door.

"Don't know, don't care." He reached an arm over his head and clawed the back of his neck.

"Could I ask a question?"

"I have the feeling you're going to ask it no matter what I say." He sighed. "So go ahead."

"Why did you run in here and take off your clothes?"

"Fleas."

"Excuse me?"

"Fleas." He scratched his chest; bright-red welts dotted his skin.

"You have fleas?"

"The suit did." He nodded at the discarded garments scattered across the cement floor.

Edie slapped a hand across her mouth. "Oh my, and I was giving you a hard time."

"Yes," he said. "You were."

"I'm so sorry. I had no idea. See, I've worked with store Santas before and I've had some unpleasant experiences."

"Are you always so quick to stereotype?" The smirk on his face told her he enjoyed her embarrassment.

"No. Listen, I'm very sorry. Let me make it up to you. I'll go find the manager and tell him about the suit." Edie felt as small as a popcorn kernel. She usually prided herself on being nonjudgmental but her reputation was riding on Santa's sobriety.

It had taken her a week of tall talking to get Mr.

Trotter to agree to hire men from the local halfway house for seasonal employment and that was after she'd already gotten approval from the store owner, J. D. Carmichael himself. Her argument that the men worked cheap was what swayed him, not her speech about community responsibility.

If Santa got soused, Mr. Trotter would hold her personally accountable. That's why she'd jumped to conclusions about his desire to run away and she was ashamed of herself.

"Before you go, would you mind doing me a favor?" he pleaded.

"A favor?" Oh heavens, what did this sexy man want from her?

"Could you scratch right here?" He twisted his arm around his back. "Right below my left shoulder blade. I can't reach the spot, and it's driving me crazy."

"Uh..." Touch this man? Her fingers ached to obey his request but her brain urged her legs to run right out the door.

"Come on, lady, have a heart."

"It's Edie."

"What?"

"My name's Edie. Edie Preston."

"That's great."

"What's your name?"

"Sam. Could you be a doll, Edie, and help me out here?"

She started to chew a fingernail but stopped herself. She'd almost broken the habit except when she was under a great deal of stress.

"Please," he begged.

"Well…"

"If you don't want to touch me then find me something to scratch with. A stick, a coat hanger. Have mercy, ma'am. Please."

Please. The magic word Edie could never resist. He certainly seemed sincere. She took a deep breath.

"Okay, I'll do it." She stepped forward and tentatively reached out a hand.

His flesh was taut and warm. He arched his back. "Higher," he instructed.

Edie splayed her fingers over his warm skin. An odd shiver zipped through her system.

"A little to the left."

Her heart thumped. She was actually touching this incredible man. Unbidden, her gaze slid down his back to the curve just above the waist band of his underpants.

What she saw was so delightful Edie snapped her eyes away and focused instead on a tower of boxes stacked in the corner.

"No," Santa turned Greek God said. "Too far. Back, back. Ah! There, that's the spot."

Edie raked her hand back and forth, keeping her eyes firmly averted.

"Harder," he said, his voice guttural. "Faster."

Geez, she needed a flame-proof suit to combat the fire building inside her.

"Yes!" He groaned. "Don't stop."

Sam bent forward slightly. Edie stood right behind him furiously scratching his naked back.

"You got it, baby!"

At that moment the storeroom door flew open. Edie and Sam turned in unison to see Mr. Jebidiah Trotter, standing in the doorway, a gaggle of rowdy kids visible behind him.

"Just what," Mr. Trotter demanded, "is going on in here?"

"I can explain," Edie said.

Mr. Trotter slammed the door behind him, crossed his arms over his chest and leveled her a condescending stare. "I suggest you begin immediately, Miss Preston, and tell me why I shouldn't fire both of you this very minute." He threw a disdainful glare in Sam's direction.

Edie raised her palms, then pulled them downward in a calming gesture. "You've got a store full of kids waiting to see Santa. If Santa doesn't appear, their mothers will take them to another department store and you'll lose business," Edie said, appealing to his mercenary side.

She didn't care for Carmichael's new manager, but she prided herself on getting along with most anyone. However, Mr. Trotter was difficult to please and wielded a heavy-handed management style, preferring punishment over positive reinforcement.

Trotter tilted his nose upward. "Be that as it may, I will not have you and your *Santa* playing sex games in my storeroom. Especially when you're suppose to be working." He tapped the face of his wristwatch.

Sex games with Santa? Edie darted at quick glance at her nearly naked partner-in-crime and gulped. Until today she had never considered Santa Claus the least bit sexy, but Sam had changed all her preconceived notions about the Christmas icon.

Sam stepped between Edie and Mr. Trotter, a thunderous expression on his face. "Listen here, Trotter, your Santa suit was infested with fleas. That's why I'm in my underwear. That's why I have welts on my body, which Miss Preston was so kindly scratching for me. If you don't get me a new suit pronto, and lay off threatening the lady, I'll be forced to report this incident to the public health department."

"You wouldn't dare." Trotter sniffed.

If she squinted just right in the glare of florescent lighting, Trotter looked exactly like the Grinch who stole Christmas—snooty nose, sour expression, virtually hairless—with an attitude to match. Edie slapped a palm over her mouth to keep from giggling.

"Try me," Sam growled, leaning forward in a menacing stance. How anyone could appear menacing in his undies, Edie didn't know, but Sam was pulling it off with the pugilistic aplomb of a heavyweight boxer. "Oh, and I believe you owe Miss Preston an apology."

"An apology? What for?" Trotter's brows plunged together in an angry V.

"Insinuating that she's the type to have a sordid affair in the storeroom."

Trotter snorted. "I will not apologize."

The two men stared each other down, eye to eye, toe to toe.

Sam clenched his hands.

Trotter's Adam's apple bobbed.

Neither blinked.

Edie's heart skipped a beat, her tummy tightened. Sam was standing up for her! No one had ever championed her like this before and while she found it thrilling, she was also terrified Trotter would fire them both. She needed her job to pay for next semester's tuition and she was certain Sam hadn't taken the position as store Santa simply for the fun of it. She had to smooth things over.

"It's all right, Sam," Edie soothed. "I know how things must have seemed—with you in nothing but your B.V.D.s and me running my hands along your..." She hesitated on the word *body*. "Why don't I go out and entertain the children before we lose customers?"

"Are you sure, Edie?" Sam asked.

"Yes." She turned to the manager. "Mr. Trotter, I give you my word, that nothing of a...er...sexual nature was going on between Sam and me, nor will it ever. I was simply trying to help him with his unfortunate flea problem.''

Mr. Trotter cleared his throat. ''Well,'' he said, ''you have been an exemplary employee until now. I guess I can give you another chance.''

He wagged a finger under Sam's nose. ''But if I even get a whiff that there is hanky-panky going on between the two of you, then you are both out on your ears. Is that understood? Carmichael's has an image to uphold.''

Edie forced a smile. ''Yes, sir, thank you. You won't regret your decision.''

Sam said nothing, just kept glaring at Trotter with a wicked stare that sent goose bumps up Edie's spine. Sam possessed the same volatile edginess of Mel Gibson's character in the first *Lethal Weapon*—one of Edie's all-time favorite movies. An edginess that appealed to the nurturer in her. She had an unexpected desire to pacify him.

''Let me see if I can find another Santa suit,'' Trotter said. ''Wait here, Stevenson. Miss Preston, back to work.'' He made shooing motions at her.

Edie ducked her head, scurried around Trotter and through the door, the bells on her hat jangling merrily. She breathed a sigh of relief, but it was only temporary. Yes, she had managed to hold on to her holiday job, but in the process she had promised to keep her hands off sexy Santa Sam.

And as luck would have it, he was the most intriguing man she'd met in years.

2

"JINGLE BELLS" jangled from the store's sound system for the nine zillionth time, as a pair of twin toddlers sat crooked in the corners of Sam's elbows, toothily drooling over his hands in surprisingly coordinated unison. He was going hoarse from too many boisterous ho, ho, hos, and his backside still itched like the dickens.

All around their little North Pole island, shoppers bustled, pushing and vying for bargains at the sales racks. The perfume counter was two aisles over, and Sam was beginning to believe the scent of rose petals was permanently imbedded inside his nostrils.

Mistletoe and holly hung from the ceiling above them, and the numerous Christmas lights strung throughout the entire tableau twinkled merrily off and on. Periodically, a nasal-voiced announcer would break in over the PA system to declare a sale on gold-plated back scratchers in bath accessories or nativity-scene decorated finger bowls in fine china.

Chief Alfred Timmons knew how to torture a guy. And surely, punishment was all this assignment amounted to because Sam didn't have a spare moment to watch the employees in order to figure out who was behind the recent rash of store thefts. Most of his investigative efforts would have to be concentrated after hours when he finished with the Santa gig every day.

He sighed. That meant twelve- and fourteen-hour workdays. Most of it spent in this red-and-white get-up. Okay. Timmons had made an impression. Sam had learned his lesson. He would never blow up the mayor's car again.

"You all look so adorable." Edie grinned. "Santa and the twins."

Sam shot her a dirty look. The woman was *way* too perky for her own good.

"Smile," instructed the twins' mother, standing off to one side.

Sam faked a smile for the kids' sake.

"Say 'fruitcake!'" Elf Edie sang out gaily, as she bent slightly to peer through the camera mounted on a tripod and clicked the shutter.

Sam blinked against the flash. At the rate he was going he'd have third-degree retinal burns by the time this day was finished. He'd already endured a litany of more than a hundred, "Santa, I wants" over the course of the last two hours. Nobody seemed to care that *Santa* wanted a potty break, a double-meat cheeseburger and a thick chocolate malt.

The twins were no more enamored of the infernal flashbulb than he. They both broke into instant tears.

"Ho, ho, ho." Sam jostled the babies, trying to quiet them. They stared into his face, then looked at each other and sobbed harder.

"I'll take them off your hands." Their mother stepped forward and relieved him of his charges.

The young mother had his complete admiration. How she dared to brave the mall alone the day after Thanksgiving with two eighteen-month-olds in tow was beyond his comprehension. The mother loaded her kids into their stroller then went over to pay Edie for the photos.

Despite his best intentions to keep his lingering glances to himself, Sam found his gaze straying down the curve of Edie's well-shaped thighs encased so enticingly in forest-green tights. She wore a red tunic sweater that just barely covered her equally well-shaped bottom.

Knock it off, Stevenson, he chided himself. *You can't get involved with her no matter how enticing the view. Don't get mixed up with people you work with. Remember Donna Beaman?*

How could he forget Donna? He'd been assigned to guard the leggy supermodel after she received death threats for testifying against a murder defendant Sam had arrested.

She'd seduced him and he'd fallen for her hook, line and sinker, to the point where he went to political functions, dressed in tuxedos and even took elocution lessons to please her. When Donna dumped him for a millionaire polo player, Sam's ego had been crushed.

What a complicated mess that relationship had become with the upshot being that one, he made it a personal policy never to get involved with co-workers or witnesses or informants, and two, he didn't get mixed up with anyone who couldn't accept him for himself, faults and all. And especially no woman who wanted to turn him into something he wasn't. He'd had enough of that from his Aunt Polly.

Still, despite his mental declaration to the contrary, he couldn't seem to stop his eyes from roving. Nothing wrong with looking at the menu, after all, just as long as you didn't order anything.

Sam tilted his head and boldly admired how the wide black belt nipped in neatly at Edie's slender waist. Sneaking peeks at this fetching, camera-wielding elf made the job tolerable.

"Got a nice tail on her don't she, Santa?"

What? Sam looked over at the next kid standing in line.

The boy was about eight with a cynical oh-yeah? expression on his freckled face. He leaned against the thick velvet rope with a cocky stance, arms crossed over his chest, legs wide apart, defiant chin in the air. The kid had no parent in attendance.

Uh-oh.

Sam had seen that same truculent stance too many times in the mirror not to recognize trouble when he spotted it. Twenty years ago he'd been the one to stand in line for the joy of heckling Santa. Paybacks were hell.

"Aren't you a little young for such talk?" Sam asked dryly, mentally casting himself back to that age.

Whenever he had acted outrageously he'd done so for one reason—attention. It had been tough growing up with an absent father and a mother who worked two jobs to make ends meet. His mother had been unable to control his rambunctious nature, and he'd run wild. Then, his mother had died of kidney failure when he was twelve. Angry at the world, he'd turned to shoplifting and petty vandalism in order to alleviate his emotional pain.

He had craved discipline, and Aunt Polly had shown up to adopt him and rescue him from himself. And while his aunt's efforts had kept him from ending up on the wrong side of the law as an adult, no matter how hard he had tried to please her, he'd always fallen short of his goal. Since his mother's death no one had loved him unconditionally.

Sam motioned to the boy. "Come here."

The kid shook his head. "No way. For all I know you're some old pervert."

"I'm Santa, kid."

"There's no such thing as Santa. You're a fraud, a fake. I'll even pull off your beard and prove it." Quick as lightning, the kid vaulted over the rope and onto the plywood sleigh. He reached out to snatch at the artificial beard but before he could grab it, Sam's fingers locked around the boy's wrist.

Sam stared him in the eye. "I'm guessing Santa didn't bring you much last year."

The boy looked startled. "There is no Santa."

"That's where you're wrong."

"Oh, yeah? Then why didn't you bring me the bike I asked for last Christmas? Why didn't you bring my daddy back home?" The boy's voice broke just a little on that last question.

"So that's what this is all about," Sam murmured. He put his arm around the boy's waist and lifted him onto his lap. The boy did not resist. "You want to tell me about it?"

The boy ducked his head and shrugged. "Nothing to tell. My dad left me and my mom. He never calls, never sends presents. My mom works real hard cleaning rooms at a motel, but she doesn't have much money. You know what I got for Christmas last year? Underwear and socks and then she took me out to a fast-food restaurant."

"That's not going to happen this year," Sam told him. "Santa's going to see to it personally. You go over there and give that pretty elf your name and address."

The boy looked at him. "Really?"

The expectant hope in his eyes hit Sam clean to the bone. He knew what it was like to be poor and unwanted. "Really."

"Gee, thanks."

"But Santa's got one request of you."

The boy rolled his eyes. "I knew there'd be a catch."

"It's not a catch. It's common courtesy."

The boy sighed. "What is it?"

"Watch your mouth and mind your mother."

"Okay." He shrugged. "I guess I can do that."

"Promise?"

"Bring me a bike and I'll do it."

The kid drove a hard bargain. Sam handed him a candy cane and watched him scurry over to Edie. A warm feeling sprouted in his chest. He had helped that boy feel better about himself and Sam would make sure the kid had a very special Christmas this year.

Edie talked to the boy, then turned to smile at Sam, an expression of awe on her fresh face. That look struck him like an arrow to the heart.

Maybe, Sam thought, *this assignment wasn't going to be so crummy after all.*

THE MORE SHE SAW OF Sam Stevenson, the more impressed and confused Edie became. He was handsome and lord, was he in great shape. He had a killer smile and infinite patience with crying babies. He'd stood up to Mr. Trotter for her, and he'd done a very nice thing giving special attention to that unhappy young boy.

So why was a guy like him playing mall Santa?

Curiosity gnawed at her.

From previous years as an elf at Carmichael's, a seasonal position she'd held all through undergraduate school and while getting her Master's degree in psychology, she knew that usually two types of men took the job. One, men so down on their luck they could only get temporary, minimum-wage work, or two, retired grandfathers who liked being around kids.

With his looks and skills Sam could easily have found a better job.

Unless he was in some kind of trouble. He denied being an alcoholic, but what about drugs? What about a gambling addiction?

Edie cast a speculative glance at him. He chatted with a little girl who wanted to know what reindeers ate so she could leave something for Rudolph and the other reindeers on Christmas Eve along with the requisite cookies and milk for Santa.

As a child, Edie had been the same, always worried about everyone and trying to make sure they were all taken care of. Her father had told her that reindeers ate Cheerios. Funny, she had thought at the time, that Cheerios was Dad's favorite cereal, too.

Sam told the little girl that reindeers loved oatmeal because it made them fly higher and faster.

What a great imagination.

Edie's inherent curiosity kicked into overdrive. He

was such a paradox. She had to know more about him and why he was working at the store.

Who knows? Maybe he is like you. Maybe he just loves Christmas. Or maybe he is going to school and needs money for tuition.

Thank heavens it was time for their prescheduled break. And maybe she would take him to lunch and sate her curiosity. She took the stand-up cardboard sign that had the face of a clock printed on it and moveable plastic hands. It said Santa Will be Back at

Edie set the time for two o'clock and posted the sign at the end of the line.

''Ready for a break?'' she asked him a few minutes later after the last child had gone through.

''You read my mind.''

''Not exactly.'' She grinned. ''My stomach's been growling for over an hour. Would you like to grab a bite to eat at the cafeteria?''

''Dressed like this?''

''Of course not. You'd be mobbed.''

''Do we have time to change?''

''We've got an hour.'' Edie pointed to the sign.

''You're an angel.'' He disembarked from the sleigh, alighting beside her graceful as a panther.

She peered at him, wondering why her heart was pounding so hard and why she had an irresistible urge to break into song. ''You've got something on your cheek.''

"Where?" He raised a hand. "Ick. Something sticky."

Edie stood on tiptoes to inspect him closer. "Looks like kid gunk."

"A lollipop-chomping little girl decided to kiss me."

"I've got some moist towelettes in my pocket. When you're working around kids you never know when one will come in handy." She retrieved a small flat package from the pocket of her tunic and tore it open. "Hold still."

Then she reached out and ran the towelette over his cheek. Her fingers trembled slightly and she felt a sudden light-headedness. She crumpled the towelette in her hand. "There. All gone."

He stared at her. Edie caught her breath. He had such beautiful blue eyes. It was strange for a dark-haired man to possess such arresting azure eyes. She was more captivated than ever.

"You've got really beautiful skin," he murmured.

"Th-thank you."

"Flawless."

"You should see the stuff I slather on my face at night." She laughed nervously.

"Now that is a tempting thought."

The idea of Sam seeing her in pj's sent a flood of heat swamping her body until she felt as if she were standing in a pool of melted butter.

MAN, but it was hot in here.

Sam gazed into those beguiling emerald eyes and knew he had to get away from Edie.

Fast.

Or he would be breaking his own rules about getting involved with people he worked with.

And that wasn't good. Not good at all.

He turned his head, and to his dismay saw a small-potatoes thug he'd arrested numerous times, coming down the luggage aisle and headed right toward him.

Freddie the Fish.

So called on the streets because he had pop eyes, fleshy folds of skin around his neck that flapped like gills when he got excited and he had such a penchant for sardines he always kept a can in the front pocket of his shirt.

Why was Freddie the Fish at Carmichael's? Freddie had been arrested, convicted and done time in prison for stealing from department store warehouses and fencing the stuff with his cousin, Walter the Weasel. Could Freddie be in cahoots with the whomever was stealing from the store?

The evidence he'd been given pointed to an inside job. The thefts had been going on for about a week. So far dresses, lawn equipment and Christmas decorations totalling ten thousand dollars had been stolen. Someone who knew the store and knew it well was smuggling the stolen items right out from under the manager's nose. No wonder Trotter was so foul tempered. Since he'd only been manager for a month, his reign was not off to a good start.

Sam frowned. It wasn't a good idea to assume anything about Freddie. For all he knew the man was merely doing his Christmas shopping.

Freddie swaggered closer.

Crud! The last thing he needed was to be fingered by Freddie the Fish.

Do something, Stevenson.

Desperate to hide his identity, Sam locked gazes with Edie, pulled her to him and dipped his head. Her sweet little mouth rounded in a startled circle.

Sam's lips were already on hers before he realized belatedly that Freddie probably wouldn't recognize him in the Santa suit.

OH! OH! His touch was incredible.

Rough, masculine fingers tenderly grazed Edie's delicate, feminine skin. Hot, firm lips scorched her mouth. Their lips interlocked like matching puzzle pieces.

Sam was kissing her!

It was probably sheer coincidence, not destiny at all but in that moment the store stereo system began playing, "I Saw Mommy Kissing Santa Claus."

Immediately, her senses zoomed into overload. *Tilt! Tilt!* The smell of him, the pressure of his body flush against hers, the intense thudding of her heart.

Her mind disengaged from her surroundings. She

forgot she was standing in the middle of Carmichael's, forgot about the multitudinous, post-Thanksgiving shoppers flowing past them, forgot about everything but Santa Sam and his dangerous kiss.

And what a kiss it was. Long, lingering and full of promise. What things would he have done with his tongue if they'd been alone?

Her stomach swooned, her cheeks flamed, her nipples tightened.

Cease and desist, Edie Renee! There will be absolutely no bursting into spontaneous combustion!

But her body completely ignored her mind's admonitions as Sam's kiss morphed her from a mild-mannered elf into a human incendiary device.

"Look Mommy, Santa Claus is kissing an elf," a child cried, pulling Edie back to reality.

"Hey, you two," a smart-mouthed teenager shouted. "Get a room."

"For shame, Santa. What would Mrs. Claus say?" someone else chimed in.

Gulping, Edie stepped back but couldn't take her eyes off him. "Wh-why did you do that?" she whispered, perplexed.

He pointed at the ceiling. "Mistletoe."

Edie looked up and sure enough, she was standing under a sprig of mistletoe. "Oh." A tree parasite had caused him to kiss her. Nothing else.

Sam took her hand. "Come on, let's get out of here. We're drawing a crowd."

Heedlessly, she allowed him to drag her into the employee lounge. Once there Edie changed in the ladies' room, Sam in the men's.

Sam emerged a few minutes later wearing a wide grin, black denim jeans and a black turtleneck sweater. His hair was combed back off his forehead, giving her full access to his gorgeous features. The man had to be the best-looking Santa Claus in the annals of department store history.

All she'd done was take off her elf hat and Merry Christmas apron, exchanged the elf shoes for brown patent leather loafers, brushed her hair and put on some lipstick. She felt as nervous and excited as a fifteen-year-old on her first date.

Calm down, Edie. You don't know anything about this guy.

Yeah, but that was the point of taking him to lunch.

"You ready?" he asked.

"Uh-huh." It was the most she could say.

He held the lounge door open for her and as they stepped into the corridor, Edie caught a glimpse of Trotter lecturing Jules Hardy, a sales clerk from cosmetics.

"Go back, go back." She turned and ran smack into Sam's chest which was solid as a brick wall.

"What is it?" Sam asked, taking her hand.

"Trotter," she said. "After what happened this

morning, I don't think it's a good idea for him to see us together.''

But it was too late to disappear back into the lounge, Trotter half turned toward them. One more second and he'd catch them holding hands.

Sam gave Edie a light push. ''You go left, I'll go right. We'll meet at the cafeteria.''

Nodding, Edie ducked down and disappeared behind a carousel of maternity dresses.

THE MINUTE she slipped away, Sam realized he'd sent her up a blind alley. She was trapped in the corner of the store with no way past Trotter.

He would have to divert the man's attention.

Sam aligned himself with a pillar decorated in red-and-white crepe paper, and stood with his arms plastered to his side, his knees clamped together. Quickly, he darted his head around the corner for a peek.

Trotter preened before a three-way, full-length mirror, licking the fingers of one hand, then combing down the few strands of hair he wore too long in a pathetic attempt to disguise his balding pate.

Turning to the other direction, Sam searched for Edie. He saw a rack of dresses ripple with movement, then spotted the top of Edie's curly head as she scurried on all fours, headed for the lingerie department.

Sam clamped a hand over his mouth to hold back the laughter.

Trotter pulled his eyes from his own reflection and

tilted his head. A frown creased his high forehead. He pivoted on his heel and walked to where Edie crouched behind a barrel of sale-priced underwear. His shoes squeaked with every step.

Creak. Creak. Creak.

Sam had to do something. He couldn't let Edie bear Trotter's disapproval alone. Stepping from behind the pillar, he called, "Mr. Trotter. May I speak to you for a moment?"

The store manager halted. "What do you want, Stevenson?"

Think, Sam. Think.

"Er…"

"Yes?" Trotter snapped. "Speak up."

Sam peered over Trotter's shoulder, searching for Edie. This was her chance to get out of the store. Where was she? "I'd like to ask about the employee discount."

Trotter frowned. "You don't get a discount. You're here to work off a community service obligation, not for a pay check."

At that moment, Edie suddenly popped to her feet about two yards behind Trotter. She waved her arms and mouthed the word, *"Go"*.

Sam shook his head at her.

"What's going on here?" Trotter demanded and snapped his neck around.

Quick as a jack-in-the-box, Edie ducked out of sight.

Trotter turned back to Sam and narrowed his beady eyes. "You're up to something, Stevenson. I've got a very bad feeling about you."

"Who, me?" Sam smiled innocently.

"Yes, you. Get back to your department." Trotter clicked his heels. "Right now."

"Uh, sir, I sorta got turned around. Could you show me where my department is?"

"Oh, for heavens sake." Trotter snorted. "Follow me."

When Trotter led the way out of ladies' wear, Sam breathed a sigh of relief. He might have looked like an imbecile but at least he'd bought Edie some time.

Why he should care, Sam couldn't say. But something about that sweet little pixie plucked heavily on his heartstrings.

3

COMMUNITY SERVICE?

Edie crouched behind the barrel of half-priced un-dies and pondered what Trotter had said. Sam was working off a community service obligation? She started to nibble a fingernail but stopped herself.

Peeking around the top of the panty barrel, she saw that Sam and Mr. Trotter had disappeared. A quick glance at her wristwatch told her they only had twenty-five minutes left for lunch. Now, with her cu-riosity about Sam stoked to high intensity, she simply had to speak to him.

"Miss Preston!"

Startled by Trotter's rapid-fire pronunciation of her name, Edie leapfrogged a foot into the air.

"Explain yourself, Miss Preston, just what are you doing on the floor in ladies' underwear?"

"Hi," Edie said perkily, peering into Trotter's un-wavering stare as if for the second time that day the store manager hadn't caught her in an embarrassing position.

"Don't give me that goody-goody smile of yours. What are you doing here?"

"I'm on my break." Edie scrambled to her feet.

Trotter rested his hands on polyester-clad hips. "Haven't you read the new policy I posted on the bulletin board in the employees' lounge this morning?"

"New policy?" Edie kept a pleasant smile on her face.

"Employees are not to roam over the store. You either stay in the lounge or in your own department. No visiting with your girlfriends in housewares, no gossiping in shoes."

"What?" Edie straightened herself to her full five-foot-two and stared the man straight in the eyes. She couldn't believe this latest outrage. According to some of the other managers, Trotter had instituted policies since he'd become manager that seemed to have no purpose beyond alienating the employees. "That's utterly ridiculous."

"Not so ridiculous, Miss Preston, when one considers that over ten thousand dollars worth of merchandise was pilfered from the store two nights ago."

"Why are you punishing the employees for shoplifters?"

"I have every reason to believe that the thieves are employees."

"You've got to be kidding." She blinked at him.

"I'm deadly serious. In fact, I'm beginning to wonder if those men from the halfway house that you talked Carmichael into hiring are behind the thefts.

They've been here a week and that's exactly how long the thefts have been going on. And, if it turns out that they are involved, I'm afraid I'll have to ask for your resignation.''

Edie opened her mouth and started to protest, then realized it was pointless arguing with the man who obviously had his mind made up. She didn't think any of the three guys she'd met during her last clinical rotation at Hazelwood Treatment Center were involved. She had truly believed in them and they had wanted so badly to go straight. That's why she'd begged first Carmichael and then Trotter to hire them. Then again, one never knew for sure.

Pensively, Edie left the department store and headed down the mall, zigzagging around the gift-laden shoppers to Lulu's Cafeteria. She hung around the door, scanning the lunchtime crowd for Sam.

''Hi,'' he murmured in her ear.

Edie whirled to face him. She hadn't heard him come up behind her. The man was as sneaky as a cat on the hunt.

''Hi yourself.''

''Hungry?'' He took her by the elbow and guided her toward the line, a medley of delicious aromas scenting the air.

''Starving.'' *For information.*

Edie tried not to be dazzled by Sam's strong fingers but her body possessed a mind of its own. Her elbow heated, then her forearm, then her shoulder and the next thing she knew every nerve ending burst, enkindled.

"Whew," she said, twisting her arm from his grasp. "It's awfully warm in here."

"Probably the heat lamps."

No, that wasn't it. What made her skin catch fire and sizzle like bacon on a hot griddle was the enigmatic Sam Stevenson.

"Here you go." He handed her a green plastic tray that was still warm from the dishwasher and smelled of industrial strength soap, and silverware rolled up in a red cloth napkin.

"Thanks."

He smiled and her knees melted. She barely managed to load her tray with tossed salad, iced tea, baked halibut, green beans and cherry pie for dessert. At the register, she fumbled in her pocket for change but Sam beat her to it. Leaning over, he paid the cashier for their meals.

"Oh," Edie protested. "I can't allow you to pay for my lunch."

"And why not?" His blue eyes danced merrily.

"Because I invited you," she argued, plucking a twenty-dollar bill from her pocket. "I'm paying."

She felt guilty letting him spend his money on her. If he was working out a community service obligation it probably meant he didn't have another job or extra cash to spare.

The cashier had already rung up their purchases and passed Sam his change.

"Wait a minute, I'm paying," Edie insisted.

"Hush, Edie, it's taken care of."

She didn't need him to take care of her. He was the one down on his luck, not the other way around. "But I insist."

"You're holding up the line." Sam picked up his tray and headed into the dining area, leaving her standing with her hands on her hips. "You can pay for lunch tomorrow," he called over his shoulder.

Lunch tomorrow? Edie thrilled to the thought. They would be having lunch together tomorrow?

Pulse slipping through her veins like high water through a dry creek bed, she picked up her tray and followed him to a table in the far corner. When she arrived, he pulled out the chair for her.

What a gentleman.

Okay, Edie Renee Preston, slow down. So he is the most fascinating, handsome man you've ever met. So he pays for your lunch and pulls out your chair for you. So he is good with kids and has the most amazing tush. He has also done something bad. Not terribly bad, of course, or he'd be in jail, but he is walking down the wrong road.

But Edie, with her abundant curiosity and her heartfelt desire to rescue anyone and anybody in need, was about to change that.

She eased into the chair. Sam leaned over to re-
move the plates and bowls from her tray.

The festive scent of his cologne teased her nose.
He smelled like Christmas—gingerbread cookies and
peppermint sticks and evergreen trees. His shoulder,
encased in that nubby wool sweater, grazed softly
against her cheek, and she drew in a deep breath.

The memory of their kiss in the midst of the
crowded department store sent a shiver of pleasure
angling through her.

Ack! What was this strange, new desire over-
whelming her?

Edie tipped her head and peeked up at him. Her
eyes focused on his lips. Darn! Why wasn't there a
nest of mistletoe hanging from the ceiling of Lulu's
Cafeteria?

After Sam put their trays away, he came back and
sat across from her. She watched with fascination as
he spread his napkin in his lap, stirred sugar into his
tea and added ketchup to his French fries.

"I want to apologize again for my behavior this
morning," she said, flattening her own napkin in her
lap. "I completely misunderstood what was happening. You know, with the Santa suit and the fleas."

He swallowed a bite of his cheeseburger before re-
plying. "No harm done."

Sam possessed perfect table manners. Unlike the
last disastrous blind date Edie had been on.

That guy had talked incessantly the entire time he'd

chewed his food, bragging how rich he'd become managing fixed-income portfolios. Edie wasn't even sure what a fixed-income portfolio manager was, but at the time it struck her that getting rich off people on fixed incomes was inappropriate. Not to mention that she'd had to repeatedly dodge the food particles he'd liberally sprayed across the table at her.

"I have a tendency to get carried away some-times," she said. "My mom tells me to be careful, that it's easy to let enthusiasm turn into zealousness. It's something I'm working on."

"I don't think you're overzealous. Just passion-ate."

Edie beamed at his compliment. "Why, thank you."

This guy was the stuff of dream dates. Except for that community service thing.

"So are you really going to buy that boy a bicycle for Christmas?"

"Sure." Sam shrugged.

"Why?"

"Why not?" Their eyes met.

"It's a lot of money and effort. Why that boy?"

"He said his father left the family, that his mother couldn't afford to celebrate Christmas. I felt sorry for him. Is that a crime?"

Sam sounded defensive. He didn't fool Edie for a moment. She knew he didn't like showing his soft side. Many men didn't. They were afraid that feelings made them vulnerable.

"May I ask you a personal question?"

"If I don't have to answer."

"How come you're working as a store Santa? I mean you don't seem the type."

Sam leaned back and draped one arm over his chair. He narrowed his eyes, quirked a smirk like a very naughty boy. "Are you sure you really want to know?"

Edie nodded.

"Even if it portrays me in a less than favorable light?"

He was going to tell her the truth. She had to give him points for honesty. "Yes."

"Court-ordered community service," he said.

"You committed a crime?"

He nodded and winked, suddenly appearing very dangerous in those dark clothes.

"What on earth did you do?" she whispered, her heart thudding a thousand miles an hour as she waited for his answer with bated breath.

"I BORROWED A CAR without permission." Sam gave her the official story supplied by Chief Timmons to Mr. Trotter.

It wasn't far from the truth. Last month, he had taken the mayor's car because he had been in hot pursuit of a drug dealer. It was his bad luck that the high-speed chase had ended when he crashed the car into a gasoline tanker truck and blew the Lexus sky high. What the mayor and Chief Timmons kept forgetting, however, was that he had nabbed the drug dealer and no one had gotten injured.

"You stole a car?" Edie stared. He hated dashing her high expectations of him. Why her opinion mattered, he couldn't say. But oddly enough, it did.

"Well, I intended on returning the car. Let's say it was something of a joy ride."

"That's not so bad."

"And then I sort of…accidentally destroyed it."

"Was the car expensive?"

"A sixty-thousand dollar automobile."

Edie winced.

"Yeah."

"Why'd you do it?" She leaned forward, fascinated by his story, her cherry pie completely forgotten.

"Boredom I guess. The judge gave me a choice. Sixty days in the county lockup or make restitution on the car and spend a hundred and twenty hours playing Santa. Not a difficult decision."

Edie shook her head. "But why did you steal the car in the first place? You've got everything going for you—looks, charm, brains. Why would you jeopardize your future for a costly joy ride? And at your age," she scolded. "It's not as if you're a misguided teen."

A certain look came into her eye. The same look he'd frequently seen on his dear old Aunt Polly's face when she'd given up her life as a missionary in the South Pacific to come home to the States and take care of him.

The ardent look of a saint intent upon saving the sinner.

"Uh, how did your wife take the news?" she asked.

He grinned, amused. So this attraction he felt was not one-sided. He'd guessed as much when he kissed her. She was fishing about his marital status. "I never made that particular mistake," he drawled, reminding himself that he would not make a mistake by acting on feelings she aroused in him.

"You consider marriage a mistake?"

He almost said for policemen, yes, but bit his tongue in time. What was it about her that made him want to spill his guts? "The divorce rate is fifty percent."

"But that means that fifty percent of the couples make it," she said.

"That's true." Edie was a glass-half-full kind-of-gal, no denying it.

She studied him a moment. "I can help you, Sam."

He leaned back in his chair and stared at her. That gorgeous mop of curly honey-blond hair, those trusting green eyes, that round, determined little chin. Sam groaned inwardly.

"Oh? I wasn't aware that I need helping."

"I have my master's degree in psychology and I'm working toward my doctorate. I do know a bit about border line personality disorders."

He couldn't suppress his smirk. "Are you diagnosing me?"

"Well, no, of course not. I don't know you well enough to do that. You've got so much going for you, and yet you do something dumb like steal a car. Why?"

"Maybe I'm just rotten to the core."

"Oh, piffle."

"Piffle?" He raised an eyebrow. "Is that some sophisticated psychological jargon?"

"You're making fun of me," she accused.

"Maybe a little." She was fun to tease; so earnest was she in her campaign to regenerate his image.

"What do you do for a living when you're not playing Santa?" she asked.

"This and that," he hedged. He didn't like to lie, even though it was often a necessary ingredient of his job. "Never could settle on one career path."

She nodded. "I suspected as much."

It was all he could do to keep from bursting into laughter. Her seriousness was genuine. She really thought she had him pigeonholed.

The woman was a reformer.

To the core.

And he was attracted to her.

That added up to serious trouble. In his current situation, Sam could not imagine a worse scenario.

The very last thing he needed was some do-gooding woman following him around telling him just how she planned to turn him into the man of her dreams—nice, respectable, home every night.

A man who looked good on paper but had no spunk, no spine, no backbone. Edie was the type who simply assumed that everyone shared her notion of the ideal home life. She was his Aunt Polly all over again—forever intent on rescuing the heathens from themselves.

He would bet a thousand bucks Edie had never done anything naughty in her entire life.

Sam knew without asking that she'd never gone skinny-dipping in the lake under a full moon. She'd never skipped school in favor of playing hooky at the local pool hall, nor had she toilet-papered the neighbors' houses on Halloween.

And Edie thought she could help him! He almost laughed aloud.

In reality she was the one crying out for life lessons. That's why she was such a crusader—taking on the flaws of others because secretly, deep inside, she was afraid to face her own rebellious nature. Which he suspected, from the kiss he'd given her, she kept tightly under wraps. She wanted to let loose, but she didn't know how.

His groin heated at the memory of their kiss. In her

lips he'd tasted so much untapped potential that he had wanted so badly to excavate. He wanted to be the one to show her just how thrillingly wicked the act of making love could be.

Unfortunately, he would not have the chance. Much as he disliked this assignment, he *was* undercover and he would not put either the investigation or Edie in jeopardy by starting a romance that he could not finish. He would not do that to either one of them. And after the investigation was over and she discovered he'd lied to her would she still be interested in him?

She reached out and placed her hand atop his. "I'm serious. I'm getting my doctorate in psychology. I can help you."

He lowered his eyelids and gave her his sexiest, come-hither stare, hoping to scare her off with raw sexuality. "Yeah?" he said in a low, husky voice. "And what if I pulled you down to my level? What if I like my life exactly as it is? What if I don't want to be saved?"

His approach paid off, rendering her to helpless stutters. "I…er…well…what I mean is…"

Reaching out, Sam stroked her jaw with a finger. She blinked, wide-eyed but did not draw back from his touch. She was so soft, so perfect. She deserved a man with a safe job, a quiet mind and a heart empty of old hurts.

"I know you mean well," he said, "but I'm way past saving."

"No one's past saving."

He wasn't the petty criminal she thought he was, but he did have his rough, wild side. A side no woman had ever been able to tame. With him, Edie was in way over her head and the cute thing about her was that she didn't even know it. Armed with a sincere smile and good intentions she marched straight into the heat of battle, never realizing she was more vulnerable than a Girl Scout in Vietnam.

From his research into Carmichael's Department Store, he already knew Edie had talked Mr. Carmichael into hiring workers from the local halfway house. Those three guys, Kyle Spencer, Harry Coomer and Joe Dawson, were his prime suspects in the thefts because they had started at Carmichaels on the very same day the first thefts occurred.

Kyle Spencer had already served a previous stint in prison after robbing a liquor store to pay for his drug habit. Harry Coomer had been on and off the wagon for years, and hung with an unsavory crowd. A DUI conviction had landed him in the halfway house. Joe Dawson had once been a decent family man, but his addictions had driven him to embezzle from his company. Any or all of them could be involved.

Why Edie had so ardently championed these three men with Carmichael and Trotter, he had no idea.

From what he'd seen of her, he didn't think Edie Preston was dumb, but boy, was she too trusting. He could tell her stories that would straighten her hair.

But why would he seek to spoil her innocent naïveté and destroy her obvious belief in her fellow man, even if he thought her deluded?

Sam looked across the table at Edie. His breath caught in his lungs. Unruly apricot curls corkscrewed around ears so delicate they appeared molded from finest porcelain. Her complexion was as smooth as creamed butter with the warm undertones of summer peaches.

And those lips! Firm, full, sweet as hand-dipped chocolate. Thanks to Freddie the Fish, he knew first-hand how incredibly kissable they were.

"We better head back," he said, before he did something really stupid like kiss her again. "We've got just enough time to change."

"Yes," She dropped both her gaze and her smile. "You're right. It's time for me to mind my own business."

Damn! Why did he feel like a schoolyard bully who'd broken the news to a five-year-old that there was no such thing as Santa Claus?

"DR. BRADDICK?" Edie rapped on her advisor's door at nine o'clock on Monday morning following the Thanksgiving holidays. She had just enough time to get her idea approved before heading to Carmichael's for another day of photographing tots and gazing into Sam's amazing blue eyes.

An idea so exciting that it had kept her awake most of the night.

The gray-haired, bearded man looked up from his desk. "Edie." He broke into an instant smile. "Lucky you caught me. I was about to leave for a conference."

"May I come in? I don't want to interrupt."

"Sure, sure." He waved at a chair. "Have a seat. You don't mind if I pack while we talk?"

"Oh, no, sir. Go right ahead."

He had an open briefcase on his desk and was filling it with books and papers. "What can I do for you, my dear?"

Edie settled her hands in her lap and cleared her throat. "I've decided to change my dissertation topic, and I need your blessing."

"Really?" He pushed the briefcase to one side so he could give her his full attention. "But I thought you had already done significant research on the subject I suggested. The long-term chemical effects of pharmacology in the psychotic brain. I even planned on including an excerpt from your work in my new book of critical thought."

"I know." Edie twisted her fingers. How to tell her instructor that his topic was…er…deadly boring to her. "But then this wonderful opportunity to do field research opened up to me."

"Wonderful? Do tell."

She met his gaze. "Dr. Braddick, I'm tired of spending my time cloistered in libraries and psychiatric hospitals and rehab centers. I'm more interested in helping ordinary people improve their daily lives than in deviant psychology."

"Since when?"

Since the beginning, Edie suddenly realized. Her admiration for her teacher's reputation had allowed her to get caught up in his vision.

"For some time now," Edie replied.

"Oh."

The dean looked so disappointed Edie had to quell the urge to rush ahead and tell him it was okay, that she would work on the dissertation he wanted her to do.

But it wasn't okay. She didn't want to write about chemicals and drugs and the tragically mentally disturbed. She wanted to study regular people who had problems that she could actually solve and without an arsenal of drugs. So she took a deep breath, plunged ahead and told him about Sam.

"I have to know why he behaves the way he does," she concluded.

Dr. Braddick sniffed. "Other than your obvious fascination with this person, what do you hope to achieve by doing a case study on him?"

"To prove that if appropriate intervention occurs at the right time in an individual's life, it can make all the difference,'' she said, her excitement growing at the thought. Edie knew she could help Sam.

"Intervention? Explain yourself.''

"Enhance his self-image through positive reinforcement. I believe I can turn him from the wrong path and show him how to reach out and take hold of the wide wonderful world that's waiting to embrace him. Hold a psychological mirror to his face, show him what he really looks like to others.''

"Do you have any idea how simplistic that sounds?'' Dr. Braddick's lips puckered as if he'd sucked on a particularly sour lemon.

For the first time Edie noticed that the bald spot atop his head had an amazing resemblance to an aerial map of Florida. Hair disappeared around Miami and didn't show up again until near Tallahassee. A large brown mole sat near Tampa.

"You think you can transform this man,'' her advisor said bluntly.

"No,'' she denied, focusing on Tampa to keep from losing her temper.

"You're a psychologist, Edie, not a missionary.'' Dr. Braddick shook his head, and a few errant strands of hair fell haphazardly across Jacksonville. "I had expected much more from you.''

"What's that supposed to mean?'' Edie frowned, irritation rising inside her. Dr. Braddick was miffed because she wasn't going to help write his book for him.

"Classic," he mumbled. "I don't want to hurt your feelings, but this is a very adolescent tendency."

"What is?"

"The eternal female need to tame the bad boy. It's the basis for romance novels, and the myth plays a prominent role in young girls' fantasies. But it has absolutely no foundation in scientific reality. Ergo, the bad boy can't be tamed."

Ergo? Who used words like *ergo* and when had Dr. Braddick gotten so darned pompous?

"I never expected you to make such broad generalizations, sir."

"And I never expected my top student to fall for a chest-thumping Neanderthal."

"I have not fallen for anyone," she denied hotly. "I merely found a subject that interested me more then the assignments you've been spoon-feeding me for the past two years."

Edie had never argued with her professor. She had been so busy groveling at the feet of Dr. Braddick's illustrious reputation, that she'd never considered that he didn't have all the answers.

They stared at each other across the desk that had become the widest chasm between student and teacher.

"Fine," Dr. Braddick said at last, the muscle in his jaw twitching with suppressed anger. "I'll allow you enough rope to hang yourself. Go ahead, engage in your case study. But don't blame me when things fall through and it costs you a wasted semester.''

Edie exhaled. "Thank you."

"But before I approve this, there have got to be some ground rules."

"All right."

"Firstly, you absolutely, positively cannot become romantically involved with this man. In any way, shape or form. If you do, your research will be tainted and you must scrap the project. Is that understood?'' He peered down at her over the tops of his reading glasses.

She nodded. "You don't have to worry about that."

"Secondly." Dr. Braddick narrowed his eyes. "This man cannot know he is the object of your study. You must observe him in secret. Otherwise, he'll alter his behavior and your results will be skewed."

"I can do that."

"And, I want a preliminary proposal on my desk the first day class resumes in the new year."

"All right."

"And, I want you to show a clear correlation between your study and how you expect to apply the results to future cases. In other words, I need to know that this project is not simply an excuse for you to get close to this man. I need concrete evidence that the interventions you use with this subject can in turn be used with other subjects to elicit constructive improvements.''

''Yes, sir.'' Edie got to her feet. ''I promise, I won't disappoint you.''

Dr. Braddick made a noise of disbelief.

She shook his hand, wished him a good trip, then left his office. As she walked through the deserted campus, past oak and pecan trees bare of leaves, a broad smile spread across her face.

''Woo-hoo,'' she shouted to the overcast sky and clicked her heels. Thanks to her interest in Sam, she'd finally had the courage to question her advisor. If just knowing him for a few days could bring this much of a change in her, what would a lifetime do?

4

Case Study—Sam Stevenson
Observation—December 2

Subject continues to work out court-appointed community service as Santa at Carmichael's Department Store. He plays the part well, remaining jovial and patient despite some minor disturbances. Including a three-year-old who unexpectedly sprung a leak on Santa's knee, and a recalcitrant elf who forgot to put film in the camera, forcing Santa to endure a half dozen do-overs.

IN HER NOTATIONS Edie did not mention that *she* was the elf in question. She closed her notebook, capped her pen and slid both into her purse.

She sat in her car outside Carmichael's with her engine idling, waiting for Sam to depart through the employee entrance. She had raced from the store ahead of him without changing clothes, hoping to get into position before he emerged.

Her heart was doing this strange little number that

oddly resembled the rumba. *Thud, thud, thud, thud, thud—thump. Thud, thud, thud, thud, thud—thump.*

What if Sam spotted her when she followed him? Where would he go after work? What would she do when he got to where he was going? These questions circled her brain like hungry vultures searching for roadside victims.

Before she had time to work herself into a full-blown frenzy, Sam exited the store looking sensational. He wore snug blue jeans that sculpted his gorgeous behind, black running shoes and a baseball jacket.

To Edie's consternation, he wasn't alone. Joe Dawson walked beside him, and they were talking animatedly.

What was Sam doing with Joe? Not that she had anything against Joe. He was a good guy when he wasn't drinking. Edie had met him in her clinical externship at the Hazelwood Treatment Center's drug and alcohol rehabilitation program. After ending up in prison for embezzlement, Joe had been serious about turning his life around and he had seemed truly grateful to Edie for getting him a job in the accounting department at Carmichael's.

Nevertheless, Edie knew that Joe was still too close to the edge, too near temptation to be hanging out with bad influences.

Like Sam?

Fretting that Sam and Joe might have too much in

common, Edie tugged off her elf hat, and tossed it aside as she watched the two men cross the parking lot and get in Joe's car.

Joe started his car. Edie put her trusty little Toyota in gear and inched after them.

Joe drove a half block and switched on his left-turn signal. Up ahead was a small shopping center that contained a liquor store, a drugstore, a hair salon, an insurance agency and a flower shop.

Don't go to the liquor store, she mentally pleaded.

Although she had no personal experience with alcohol abuse, as both a psychology major herself and the daughter of a social worker and a Presbyterian minister, Edie had met people with substance abuse problems.

The experiences had made an impression on her. She had never touched a drop of alcohol in her life. Not that she thought any less of those who did take a drink now and then. Plenty of people could imbibe and be none the worse for it. But not Joe Dawson.

And Sam?

Edie's gut tightened.

Joe stopped the car outside the drugstore. Edie allowed herself a relieved sigh, then immediately wondered what they were buying and decided to follow them into the building.

The two men got out of the car.

Edie parked a safe distance away and watched them disappear inside.

Well, she wasn't going to find out anything lurking in the car but what if she followed them in and they spotted her?

So what? It was a free country. She didn't owe them any explanation. She could shop in the drugstore just as readily as they.

Her mind made up; Edie left the car and scurried inside.

The heat in the overcrowded building stifled her senses. Edie wished she'd left her coat in the car. She glanced down first one aisle and then another.

No Joe. No Sam.

Rats.

She walked past first aid supplies, past cosmetics and soaps. She dodged a group of gray-haired ladies arguing over which was the most flattering color of Miss Clairol and skipped around a clutch of uniformed schoolgirls giggling about the nine hundred varieties of blemish cures.

She caught sight of Sam standing at the pharmaceutical counter at the back of the store. Edie screeched to a halt and turned her back to him. Ducking her head, she walked backward to the end of the aisle one baby step at a time, until she stood just a few feet away. Luckily, she remained hidden from view behind a cardboard cutout of some famous athlete extolling the virtues of his favorite brand of jock itch cream.

She was out of Sam's sight, but within hearing

range. The suspense was killing her. What kind of prescription was he getting filled?

The pharmacist mumbled something.

Sam laughed.

Edie cocked her head to one side. Straining, she leaned farther back.

Her heel caught the athlete's life-size cutout, and he began to totter. Desperate to keep out of sight, Edie reached to steady the grinning cardboard effigy.

And lost her balance in the process.

Her elf shoes skidded on the waxed floor. One knee buckled and the leg went shooting out beneath her.

Flailing, she desperately grabbed for a shelf in a vain attempt to remain standing and wrapped her fingers around the metal rack.

For one miraculous instant the rack held.

Then, just when she thought she had everything under control, the smug, artificial athlete slowly toppled onto her shoulders.

The straw that broke the camel's back.

Edie's remaining leg gave up the battle. The thin rack collapsed under the full brunt of her weight.

She sank to the floor, crushing Mr. Jock Itch underneath her.

The contents of the shelf showered down. Boxes and boxes of condoms.

A dozen different brands. Viking. White Knight. Sir Lancelot.

Color condoms. Ultra-thin condoms. Ribbed-for-her-pleasure condoms.

A clerk shouted in dismay.

People rushed over.

Edie felt a blush heat her cheeks and spread to tingle her scalp. Looking down, she saw she held a box of condoms in her hands.

Neon. Bargain count—fourteen for the price of twelve. Jumbo size.

"Edie? Are you all right?"

She heard Sam's voice and wished at that moment that she was naked on Interstate 12 doing the tango with a dancing gorilla. It would have been far less embarrassing.

"I'm fine," she managed to say.

"You're sure?" he insisted, helping her to a sitting position. His hand lay pressed against her back and all she could do was wish him away.

"Great. Never been better. I wreck drugstores all the time. It's a little hobby of mine."

She tried not to look at him, but he cupped a palm around her chin and she found herself gazing into those compelling blue eyes.

"Well then, sweetheart," he said, gently prying the box of condoms from her hand and tugging her to her feet, "if you're planning that big of a Christmas party maybe you should have these things delivered."

HE HADN'T MEANT to tease Edie about the condoms.

If Sam was being completely honest with himself, he would admit he was jealous.

Who was she buying those condoms for?

What was more important, why did he care?

She wasn't married. Joe Dawson had told him that. Another thing that had irritated Sam was the admiration evident in Joe's voice when he spoke about Edie. He had been lauding her virtues since they'd left the drugstore. Clearly, the guy had a major jones for her.

That knowledge didn't improve Sam's mood much.

''Turn right,'' he told Joe.

''Sylvan Street?''

''Uh-huh.''

They drove past an odd combination of houses in the ethnically mixed neighborhood of Jameson Heights. Hundred-year-old, multifamily Victorians sat on lots next door to newly built adobe structures. This house had a tile roof, that one had pink flamingoes in the yard.

Sam had grown up here at a time when the area was rough-and-tumble. He liked the cultural diversity. On warm evenings in the summer, one could walk down the sidewalk and smell dinners cooking in an exotic mix of spices: curry and cumin, anise and fennel, garlic and oregano.

From one window would come a throbbing salsa beat, from another the wail of a blues guitar. There might be a low-rider parked in one driveway, a Harley in another, a brand-new Volkswagen Beetle in a third.

"Here's my place." Sam pointed to the frame house built in the fifties that he had recently renovated himself.

Joe pulled into the driveway. "Do you need a ride to work tomorrow?"

"No, thanks. My car should be out of the shop."

Joe nodded. "Hey, maybe you'd like to go out with me and Kyle and Harry a week from next Saturday night. Harry's girlfriend is headlining at a gentleman's club over on Ashbury. You interested?"

Sam pricked up his ears. This is what he'd been angling for when he'd befriended Joe the afternoon before, then asked him for a ride to work. "Sounds like a fun time," Sam said, as he got out of the car with the bag of prescriptions he'd picked up at the drugstore for his Aunt Polly.

"See ya at work." Joe put the car in gear and backed from the driveway.

Sam waited a moment then walked across the street to his Aunt's house. He rang the bell. "Got your pills," he said, when she opened the door.

Even in her early seventies, Aunt Polly still possessed the same military posture from her youth. She reached out and took the sack. "Good boy, Sammy," she praised.

When he did what she wanted, his aunt lauded him with compliments but let him step out of line and she lashed him with the sharp side of her tongue. Even now, at age twenty-nine he was unable to escape her chiding. He'd learned to live with it. He loved her after all, in spite of everything.

"I always knew if I chewed on you long enough you'd turn out to be a good boy. Course it took a whole lot of chewing." She chuckled. "You certainly had a mind of your own. Always had to do things your way, and the rules be damned."

"How's the arthritis today?" he asked, not all that interested in cataloguing his faults.

She made a face, held up her gnarled fingers. "Don't ask. You want to come in? I've got soup cooking."

"Thanks for the invitation, but I've got work to do."

"Work, work, work. When are you going to settle down and get married?" His aunt shook her head. "If you don't give me grandnieces and grandnephews soon, I'll be too old to play with them."

"Ha! That'll be the day."

"I'm serious, Sam, you need somebody to watch out for you."

That was the last thing he needed. "I promise." He leaned over to kiss his aunt's dry cheek that smelled of lanolin. "When and if I decide to get married, you'll be the first to know."

After bidding her goodbye, he trotted back across

the street to his house. The place seemed unnaturally silent, unusually empty.

To heck with self-pity. Sam turned the television on a bit too loud, trying to drown out his loneliness.

Marriage. Aunt Polly seemed to think that was a cure. Never mind that she'd never married herself.

Truthfully, he was too busy for marriage. He often worked long, dangerous hours. He'd seen too many police officers' marriages fail for those very reasons. Sam had decided maybe he wasn't the marrying kind. Why should he surrender his independence?

A lump formed in Sam's throat. Yes. It would take someone pretty darn special to get him to the altar. His fantasy woman would have to accept him for who he was, a stomach-scratching, bad-joke-telling, junk-food-loving caveman. She would not try to force him into some ridiculous mold the way Donna had.

An old embarrassment flared in him. Why had he allowed Donna to manipulate him? When in love, his self-respect seemed to fly right out the window.

No more.

In the past love had twisted him into shapes he didn't fit. He wasn't a hunk of pasta dough ripe for the press of some woman's choosing. He wasn't fancy. No rigatoni or farfelle or mafalda. He was elbow macaroni, slightly bent, but down to earth.

And then, for absolutely no reason whatsoever, he thought of Edie Preston.

Sweet Edie with the face of an angel and a ditzy,

interfering, endearing personality that made you want to hug her and swat that round little bottom at the same time.

Right now she was probably making love to her boyfriend.

Sam ground his teeth.

Damn. He had a job to focus on. Thieves to catch. A penance to pay so he could return to real detective work. Some pixie with a smile that rocked his world, wasn't going to distract him.

Too bad she had the most stellar pair of legs he'd ever seen and a chest that could rivet any man's gaze. Too bad she possessed eyes as green as deep summer. Too bad she was so innocent.

She deserved some socially conscious, human rights activist to a world-weary guy whose life revolved around dangerous criminals, perilous risks and touchy situations.

Unlike Edie, Sam had no illusions about changing the world. He was a cop because he enjoyed seeing justice done, not because he was out to save humanity.

If he ever fell in love he wanted a tall, muscular woman who could protect herself. A practical-minded woman who accepted the world as it was and didn't expect him to be something he wasn't. Not a bit of fluff who tried to change his basic personality at every turn.

Unfortunately Christmas was still over three weeks

away. Could he resist her until the twenty-fifth? Or better yet, could he solve the thefts before then?

Tomorrow, he'd go into the store early. Chief Timmons had gotten him a key from J. D. Carmichael. He would snoop around, and see if he could unearth anything on his own time. Playing Santa wasn't getting him anywhere, especially since he couldn't seem to keep his eyes off a certain charming elf.

If he didn't watch himself, if he didn't keep his guard piled higher than the Great Wall of China, Sam feared he could fall for Edie Preston.

Fall hard enough to shake the plaster on his rebellious self-image.

For a man who had spent his entire life trying to prove that he was too tough for mushy stuff like love, that would never do.

THE WAY Sam had called her sweetheart. In that deep sexy tone. Edie sprinted around the upper level of the mall, unsuccessfully trying to focus on anything but Sam and the previous day's humiliation. She'd spent the entire night tossing, turning and thinking about Sam. Around dawn she had come to one conclusion. She still wanted to do a case study on him. He was her sphinx. The riddle she had to solve. The enigma she must crack. If she could come to understand the real Sam Stevenson, Edie felt she could understand anyone.

How she was going to face Sam again after yesterday's fiasco at Serve-Rite Drugs?

Edie cringed.

He would look at her and think—Glow in the dark condoms. Jumbo size. Then, just like any virile, red-blooded American male, that thought would lead to another and his mind would ride the sensual track, only a mental hop, skip and jump to picturing her naked.

Her face flamed.

Head down to cover her impending humiliation, she pumped her arms and legs faster, propelling herself around the mall's upper level, desperate to outrun her folly.

She approached a side entrance near Carmichael's, and from the corner of her eye, caught a glimpse of someone striding through the door. She tried to slow up and put on the brakes but it was too late.

She slammed into the back of a tall, broad-shouldered man.

''Whoa, there.''

A hand reached out and wrapped around her waist, holding her close, holding her safe.

That voice. That touch. That unique masculine scent.

It couldn't be. She looked up and blinked.

But it was.

Talk about Murphy's Law. Talk about being in the

wrong place at the wrong time. Talk about the fickle hand of fate.

She was cursed. Doomed to continually disgrace herself whenever she was around him.

Sam. Standing before her, big as day and twice as nice.

Inwardly, she groaned, as if he didn't already consider her the world's biggest klutz. He was probably beginning to think she had some kind of medical condition.

"Edie?"

"Sorry about rear-ending you," she blabbered, then realized how that sounded.

"Try keeping your head up when you're power walking," he said, chucking a finger under her chin, and sending a fissure of pure sexual energy sizzling through her. "It'll cut down on mishaps."

"Th-thanks," was all she could stammer in return.

"Don't mention it." He smiled and she found herself lost at sea in his eyes.

"What are you doing here so early?" Edie glanced at her watch. "The store doesn't open for another hour."

"Uh…" Sam hesitated and dropped his gaze.

In that instant, Edie knew he was about to lie to her and her heart plummeted into her sneakers.

"Er…I'm meeting someone."

If he'd been Pinocchio, his nose would be punching her in the chest right about now.

"Someone?"

"Joe Dawson. He gave me a ride home last night. My car is in the shop and in return I told him I would help him with his, um…"

"Yes?" Edie could see him searching his mind for a plausible excuse. His deception upset her.

Why Sam, why?

"His taxes."

"Joe's an accountant," she pointed out.

A desperate expression crossed his face. "Uh, I know but I have an investment he's interested in as a tax shelter."

"You don't have to lie to me, Sam," she said softly. "If you don't want me to know something, tell me that it's none of my business."

"Edie…" He reached out to her but she stepped away.

"It's okay. For whatever reason you feel compelled to steal cars and lie. I'm not judging you. I'm just curious as to why you feel the need to do things that are detrimental."

"I'm sorry," he said. "You're right. There are things I can't explain to you."

"You don't owe me any explanations but you do owe it to yourself, Sam, to question your own behavior."

"I'm not what I seem to be."

"No," she replied, "you're not."

That was why she found him so mesmerizing. Was

Dr. Braddick correct? Was she under the spell of nothing more than a woman's age-old desire to tame the bad boy? Was she so gullible as to believe she could change this man who oozed potential and yet seemed so eager to throw it all away in the pursuit of macho thrills?

Nonsense. She would prove to both herself and Dr. Braddick that Sam was worth saving and she was just the psychologist to do it.

5

Ida ibidigi aquanga. Maco ao under she spoil of
military more and a woman's anges. I'd cario comar
iki and na?y Moy she shiull be as io balieve she
cadd i cagon am so way a mach primual and yet
pround to ben ala malar ay is shu presunn
nadi simla, i wo agbleky arahandi
bas ciur na ai wuuld guna ta tonk hatell and Dr
Ship asis has bua muy woald saww: mad he was ha
abil

EDIE COMPLETELY unnerved him.

The expression of disappointment in her eyes sent him hurtling back to his childhood when he'd had to face Aunt Polly after being collared by the store detective for shoplifting a screwdriver at Bunson's Hardware.

What had begun as a humiliating experience had in the end turned into an interest in police work. The officer who'd come to the store had a long talk with him about right and wrong and in the end Sam had joined the afterschool, community basketball team sponsored by local law enforcement. Because he had admired and respected the officer so much, Sam had become a policeman himself.

Unfortunately, he couldn't explain that to Edie. What troubled Sam was how badly he wanted to tell her that he was an undercover cop, not a two-bit criminal serving out court appointed community service as she believed. But he could not because it put her in jeopardy.

Forget her, Stevenson, and get on with your job.

It was bad enough he'd been thinking about Edie

so intently that morning, that he'd accidentally locked his keys in the car. Why couldn't he get the woman off his brain?

Today, he planned on befriending another man from Joe's halfway house, Kyle Spencer. Kyle, a mechanic by trade, had been hired at Carmichael's as a maintenance worker one week ago, and he was currently dating fellow employee, Jules Hardy.

Besides using his investigative skills in an attempt to discover if Kyle might be involved in the thefts, Sam hoped the man had a Slim Jim he could borrow to break into his locked vehicle.

He tried to concentrate on his work, both as Santa and as undercover cop. He bounced kids on his knees, all the while keeping his eyes on the crowd. He skipped lunch and instead hung around the parking lot talking to the employees who sneaked out for a smoke, surreptitiously asking questions about their colleagues.

Yet no matter how hard he struggled to keep his mind on track, time after time Sam felt his attention irresistibly drawn to Edie. He loved the way she smiled at the children, and the way she hummed Christmas songs under her breath. He adored the way she smelled like warm chocolate chip cookies fresh from the oven and the way she made his groin tighten whenever she occasionally brushed against him.

His desire for her was nonsensical and he knew it. Pure animal attraction had never overwhelmed him like this before, but he would not succumb to this driving urge to nibble those full cherry lips again. He would not.

He could resist.

At that moment, Edie dropped a roll of film not two feet from him. She bent over to pick it up favoring him with an up-close-and-personal view of the world's most spectacular behind.

Sam gritted his teeth. He could resist.

Well, he *could!*

Case Study—Sam Stevenson
Observation—December 8

Subject hangs around the department store long after his shift has ended. Why? Today, a thousand dollars worth of tools were discovered missing from the hardware section. Early this morning, subject was seen in that area of the store, clearly violating the new store policy against loitering in other departments. Could there be a connection between subject and the missing tools?

EDIE NIBBLED on the end of her pen, then crossed out the last sentence. Conjecture had no place in an objective case study; yet, she couldn't help wondering. Was Sam involved with the stolen tools? She didn't want to believe it, but something told her he was not all that he seemed.

Little things gave him away. The furtive manner in which he kept glancing around the store at the oddest times as if he expected a burly policeman to tap him on the shoulder. The way he would suddenly disappear leaving Edie to entertain the waiting children until he returned.

One thing was clear; she had to follow Sam again.

Feeling like a cast member from *Mission Impossible,* Edie mentally played the theme song in her head as she sat slouched in the front seat of her Toyota Tercel, waiting for Sam to appear.

A shiver ran through her and she snuggled deeper into her coat. She thought of letting the engine idle and running the heater, but she'd just bought a book called, *How to Find Out Anything About Anybody.* The author suggested when tailing someone it was best to remain as unobtrusive as possible and that meant not running your car engine despite the cold.

She glanced at her watch. Over forty minutes had passed since the end of their shift.

Joe Dawson came and went. Still no Sam. Just when she'd decided to call it quits, Sam emerged from a side door and headed for a classic red Corvette parked in a far corner. He hesitated a moment, casting a furtive glance first left, then right. Then he pulled something from his hip pocket.

What was he doing?

Edie twisted around and grabbed the binoculars

resting on the back seat. Bringing the field glasses to
her eyes, she studied him.

He held a straight metal object in his hand and he
was feeding it alongside the car window and down
into the driver's side door.

Her heart catapulted into her throat.

No! No! He couldn't be stealing that red Corvette.
Not right before her very eyes.

But it seemed that he was.

In less than a minute he had the door open, then
he quickly glanced around again before climbing inside. He bent his head low over the dash so that she
could barely see the top of his head.

She watched cop shows. She knew he was hot-
wiring that car.

"For shame, Sam Stevenson," she lectured.
"Haven't you learned anything from your stint in
community service?"

Apparently not.

The Corvette roared to life, a puff of exhaust shooting from the tailpipe. He slipped the car into gear and
pulled out of the parking lot.

Oh! He was getting away.

Edie tossed the binoculars into the seat beside her,
started her own engine and took off after him.

Hang on Sam! I'll help you!

She gunned the Toyota, whizzed past a station
wagon filled with startled nuns, changed lanes and
slid in behind Sam, careful to keep two cars sand-

wiched between them. They chugged along at seventy in a fifty-five-mile-per hour zone.

Going so fast set Edie's teeth on edge. She obeyed the laws of the land. She didn't speed, she didn't litter and she certainly didn't steal cars.

She did like helping her fellow man, and if saving Sam from himself meant a few measly traffic violations then she would accept responsibility for her actions.

Just when she was thrilling to life in the fast lane, Sam took the Jameson Heights exit ramp and pulled into the driveway of a white-frame house, circa 1950s, with green shutters on curtained windows. No lights shone through. Edie pulled over to the curb where she was, three houses down from him, and parked.

What was he doing here? Whose house was this? She feared the answers to those questions. Mostly, she feared what dark things she might discover about this mysterious man.

He got out of his car, walked up the steps, reached in his pocket for a key, opened the door and went inside.

Did he live here?

Hmm.

Had he stolen this car only to bring it home?

Edie frowned and experienced a strange letdown. What had she expected? That he would take it to a chop shop? Drive to the Mexican border? Meet Joe Dawson somewhere in a clandestine exchange?

Yes. Yes. And yes.

Maybe he was stopping off to pick up something and would be on his way in a few minutes.

A light came on in the house. Edie put the binoculars to her eyes. She couldn't see much from this distance. Through the half-opened curtains she spotted a couch, caught a glimpse of a television set.

A shadow passed before the window.

Sam.

And he'd taken his shirt off.

His bare chest glistened in the muted lighting. It looked as if he were heading for the shower.

Edie inhaled sharply and almost choked on her breath. She coughed, gasped. Even from this distance the man had the power to disrupt her oxygen supply.

Resolutely, she turned her mind and her eyes away from the sight of his naked torso. As Edie sat pondering the question of what to do next, she happened to glance in her review mirror. A patrol car rolled slowly down the road toward her.

Her heart scaled her throat.

Don't panic. Don't assume anything, Edie told herself, but her palms were suddenly sweating enough to fill a ten-gallon bucket.

And in her heart, she knew. Someone had reported the red Corvette stolen. Someone had witnessed Sam stealing it from the mall parking lot.

The police were on to him.

The car inched closer, passed Edie. The driver was a Denzel Washington look-alike, his gaze trained on Sam's house. On the red Corvette.

Edie's pulse leapt like a tiger lunging at the bars of its cage. She had to warn Sam. So determined was she on helping him, she didn't stop to consider the consequences of her actions.

She stumbled from the Toyota, raced down the property line of the house beside her and into the backyard. She couldn't let the patrolman see her.

Darn! There was a six-foot privacy fence between this house and the one next door.

Edie drew a deep breath and got a running start at the fence. Someone inside the house pushed open the sliding glass door and yelled at her but she was already over the fence and into the yard next door.

She was still two houses away from Sam, separated this time by a chain-link fence and a really big German shepherd lying on the back porch.

The animal lifted his head and uttered a low, menacing growl.

She yelped and sprinted forward.

The dog charged.

The chain-link fence clanked nosily as her feet found toe holes.

The dog lurched.

Edie squealed and felt teeth sink into her rear end.

She heard a loud ripping noise when she pulled free and tumbled over the fence.

She fell and scraped her palms, but she didn't take time to assess her wounds. Thankfully, this last house had no fence. She could see Sam's backyard from here.

Her breath coming in short, quick gasps, she turned her head toward the street, and saw that the patrol car had pulled to a stop beside Sam's house.

Hurry. Hurry.

On winged feet, she flew up the stone steps and pounded on Sam's back door with both fists. "Sam, Sam," she shouted. "Get out here, now."

He didn't answer.

Oh, no! Had the cop already taken him away?

She pounded again. Harder this time. "Sam!"

The back door jerked open. Edie tumbled inward to see Sam standing dripping wet and totally naked save for the narrow strip of towel wrapped around his waist.

His eyes widened. A smile curled at the corner of his lips. "Edie? What are you doing here?"

The front doorbell rang.

It had to be Denzel.

And Sam was nearly naked in thirty-degree weather. Oh, no!

She grabbed his hand and tugged him out the back door. Never mind his undressed state. She would get him to the car, and crank up the heater to warm him.

She'd take him to her house. They could talk and decide how to extricate him from this mess.

''You've got to get out of here. Now.''

''Wait. Slow down. What's going on? I just got out of the shower.'' He looked completely perplexed.

Despite the urgency of the moment, Edie couldn't help noticing how the terry cloth towel clung damply to his tanned, muscular body, nor could she keep her eyes from tracing the whorl patterns of dark chest hairs. Heck, even his long bare toes were cute.

Stop this, Edie. You can't let physical attraction deflect you from your purpose. Forget Sam's good looks. Remember that he's your dissertation project. Professionals do not become involved with their subjects.

''What's going on?'' he repeated, dragging her back to the present moment.

''A policeman is at your front door. You're about to be arrested,'' she said, still yanking on his arm. ''Come with me. My car's parked out front. We'll have to go the back way, and I can tell you from experience that German shepherd in house number two is a real meanie. If we hurry. I can get you out of this. At least for the time being.''

He stared at her as if she'd stepped off a spaceship.

Maybe she'd been talking too fast and he hadn't understood the urgency of the moment.

The doorbell pealed again.

"Excuse me, Edie." He turned and started back into the house.

"No!" She clung to him like super glue. "Not unless you want to go to jail."

"Go to jail?" His eyes were laughing but he kept his mouth perfectly straight. He thought she was joking. "For what?"

"For stealing that red Corvette parked in your front driveway."

Sam's mouth twitched, then he tossed his head back and the sound of laughter rolled from him like gathering thunder.

Edie frowned. "What's so funny?"

"That's my car."

"Don't you lie to me, Sam Stevenson. I saw you break into it. I saw you hot-wire the thing in the parking lot."

He wiped tears from his eyes with the back of a hand and chuckled that much harder.

Edie sank her hands on her hips. She didn't understand this man. Not one bit. "You won't be laughing when that Denzel Washington look-alike cop on your front step has you in handcuffs. This is serious."

"So it's my neighbor Charlie at the front door? Come on in. Close the door. Have a seat. I'll be right back." Sam twisted the towel tighter around his waist then padded down the hall to the front door.

Confused, Edie stepped inside and pulled the door

shut behind her. It wasn't a figment of her imagination. She *had* seen Sam break into that car.

Muted male voices were discussing something in the hallway.

Edie tiptoed forward and tilted her head, hoping to overhear their conversation.

The front door clicked closed.

Footsteps sounded.

Edie darted back to the kitchen table and plunked into a chair.

"Yeow!"

She shot to her feet, her hand at her backside. Her pants were ripped, her skin nipped. That German shepherd had nicked her and she'd been so intent on warning Sam, she had forgotten all about it.

"What's wrong?"

Sam's tall frame filled the doorway, concern for her etching his face.

She swallowed. Hard. She forgot all about the dog bite. Her gaze traveled from his broad shoulders, down his impeccable chest to where the dark hairs on his belly disappeared into a V where he kept his towel closed with a mere thumb and forefinger.

Sucking in a deep breath, Edie realized only that thin scrap of terry cloth stood between her and glory. If Sam's fingers were to slip…

"What did Denzel want?" she asked, moistening her lips with the tip of her tongue.

A smile tugged his mouth upward. "To invite me to his Christmas party."

"Oh."

"I heard you cry out in pain just now," Sam said. "Is something wrong?"

Edie fingered her torn pants. "I sort of had a run-in with your neighbor's German shepherd."

One eyebrow shot up on his forehead. "Snookems?"

"Two houses over." She poked a thumb in the direction she'd come from. "I think he won the argument."

"Let me see."

Edie's gaze flicked to his towel once more. "Maybe you better put on some clothes first."

"Yeah," he said and darn if his voice didn't sound husky. "I'll be right back."

"Take your time."

He wasn't gone for long but it didn't take many minutes for Edie to feel foolish. In her mind's eye she retraced her steps, relived her mistakes.

She dropped her face into her hands. He probably thought she was nuttier than a pecan tree at harvest time.

Then she realized she was missing a prime opportunity to get to know him better. Tidy kitchen. No dirty dishes in the sink, no toast crumbs on the counter like at her place. The color scheme was masculine, black and white and chrome. Black-and-white checkerboard pattern on the tile floor, black counter-top, white cabinets, chrome appliances.

Getting up, she opened the refrigerator door as qui-etly as she could and took stock. Ah, now, here was proof a rebel lived here. One can of beer, ketchup, a carton of Chinese takeout.

Nosily, she opened the carton of Chinese food. Beef lo mein. Her favorite.

"Hungry?" Sam asked. "I can call for a pizza if you want me to."

"No." She shook her head and put the lo mein back on the shelf. "I've got to be going." Before she did something totally idiotic like jeopardize her dis-sertation.

He wore blue jeans and a Dallas Cowboys sweat-shirt. In his hand he held a bottle of hydrogen per-oxide, antibiotic ointment and a box of adhesive ban-dages. "Let's take a look at that wound."

This was humiliating. Edie turned and favored him with a view of her bottom.

Sam stepped closer and squatted level with her backside. "The pants are goners, I'm afraid."

She felt his fingers touching her skin through the tear. Closing her eyes, she fought back her natural feminine responses to being touched by a man she found very handsome by reminding herself repeatedly that she was a psychologist. Sam needed her help. She would not compromise either her case study or his future mental health for the sake of a little physical attraction.

"The bite's not bad. Hardly any blood at all. Snookems barely broke the skin, but I imagine you're going to have a bruise in the morning. Good thing I know the dog's had his shots."

"Good thing," Edie echoed.

"Could you bend over the table so I can doctor this?"

"Uh, sure."

"This might sting."

The hydrogen peroxide was cool, countering the sudden heat in the room. Next came the ointment, then the bandage. It seemed an eternity passed before he said, "There. All done."

She straightened, and spun away from him as quickly as she could. "Thank you."

"No. Thank you."

"For what?"

"Risking life and limb to warn me."

"You're not angry that I thought you were stealing another car?" She peeked at him.

His eyes crinkled at the corners when he smiled. "A natural mistake. What impresses me is that you cared enough to follow me home and then endangered yourself for my sake."

She shrugged, feeling guilty. She couldn't tell him ulterior motives had possessed her to shadow him.

"I'd hate to see you get into any more trouble," she said. That was certainly true. No lies there.

He took a step toward her. "I'm not a project, Edie."

Project? Had he guessed that she was using him as a case study? But how could he know that?

She laughed nervously. "I never said you were."

"I can see it in your eyes. You're like my Aunt Polly, just like my old girlfriend. You take one look at me and see a 'fixer-upper'. Well, I'm not some run-down house, lady. I'm a man." He took another step. The floor creaked beneath his weight. "With both strengths and flaws."

"I never…"

"Shh." He raised a finger, pressed it against her lips. "I've seen a lot of life. A lot of ugly things I pray you'll never see."

Edie gulped.

"Your bright, optimistic outlook on the world is one of the things I like about you. But Edie, you've been too sheltered. Yes, maybe you spent your life helping out at homeless shelters and counseling alcoholics but it's always been secondhand. You could perch a safe distance away and give out advice without having to get your hands dirty."

"I resent that." Her temper flared. Who was he to judge her?

"Come on, admit it. You've never done anything bad, have you? You don't break the rules. You never came in late after your parents' curfew. You've probably never even gotten a parking ticket.''

''Well, Mr. Smarty, you'd be wrong. I did something bad once.''

''Oh?'' He smirked, irritating her even more. Just because she didn't lie and cheat and steal didn't mean she hadn't lived. ''What terrible crime did you commit?''

''I forgot to return a library book. They sent me a notice that said if I didn't pay for it they were going to issue a warrant for my arrest,'' she confessed.

Sam threw his head back and laughed at her for the third time that evening. Long. And hard.

Edie bristled. ''It wasn't funny!''

''I'm sure it wasn't to you. And I'm also sure you burned rubber getting to the library as fast as you could to pay that fine.''

''You're not being fair.''

''No, Edie, you're the one who's not being fair. Until you've walked a mile in my shoes, don't assume anything about me and don't try to save me, okay?''

She stared at him. He was right. The outside world hadn't really touched her. Because of her parents and their occupation, because of her own chosen field, she'd always been the one to give advice, to lend a helping hand. But in all honesty did she really know what she was talking about? Who was she to give him advice? She'd never been poor, never gone without food, never lived without a roof over her head.

"Before you're ever going to relate to your patients, before you can ever really understand people, you're going to have to take a walk on the wild side, Edie Preston."

"A walk on the wild side?"

"Face your temptations. Acknowledge your demons."

This didn't seem the time to point out she had no demons. No temptations.

Except one.

The urge to help others exorcise *their* demons.

She studied him. This sexy, dangerous man with a steel jaw and the ability to excite her like no other. In that moment Edie knew there was another temptation in her life. One she had been avoiding for a very long time.

6

SAM TOOK a step toward her.

Edie backed up, until she bumped flush against the kitchen wall, her eyes widening.

He had one goal on his mind.

Kiss those lips. Kiss her silly. Scare her off. Make her go away. Before she interfered in his investigation. Before she interfered in his life.

Already, she was coming too close. Following him, warning him about the cops, trying to psychoanalyze him.

The woman was nothing but trouble. She looked at him with bright, admiring eyes. She saw him as a knight in slightly dented armor. Armor she aimed to polish to a high shine.

He'd seen the look. Once a crusader, always a crusader. He couldn't change her any more than she could change him. Not that he even wanted to change her. Her earnestness, sincerity and concern for others captivated him, but being attracted to a woman like Edie and living with one were two very different things indeed.

One way or the other he had to get rid of her and

kissing her seemed the most pleasant method to achieve his purpose.

"I could teach you to walk on the wild side," he murmured, coming closer and resting his forearm on the wall above her head. If his most forward moves didn't make her run for the hills, nothing would.

Edie blinked.

He lowered his head along with his voice, and never took his eyes from hers. "I'd enjoy teaching you." He reached out a hand, softly traced a finger around the neck of her blouse. Her body trembled at his touch.

She squared her shoulders, took a deep breath and drew herself up tall. "At this juncture in your life don't you think it would be more constructive if you concentrated on changing your self-defeating behavior patterns rather than trying to seduce me?"

"Do you?" He dipped his head lower still until their lips were inches apart.

"Yes." She nodded her head vigorously. "I do. You're using sexual overtures as a way to avoid dealing with your own shortcomings."

"Am I?"

"Yes."

"How do you know I'm not just hot for you? Sometimes doctor, a cigar is only a cigar."

"Are you trying to intimidate me with your sexuality?"

Yes.

"You mean like this?"

Then he wrapped his arms around her waist, pulled her to his chest and kissed her like he had been aching to kiss her since his lips had brushed hers that very first day at Carmichael's.

Man, did she ever taste good. Like honey and dew-drops and sweet, sweet sin. Her breath hammered in his ear, her soft scent curled in his nostrils.

He shouldn't have kissed her. Not even to scare her off. He was rock hard and growing harder by the moment. His veins filled with heated tension. It had been a long time since he had made love to a woman and his body was well aware of that fact.

You can't make love to Edie, he told himself. *You're an undercover cop, and she thinks you're a hapless screwup. You're too set in your ways to be reformed. You're rough-cut, she's fine china. There's a hundred million reasons this can't continue.*

"Sam," she whispered into his mouth.

"Yes, sweetheart?"

"Please get your hands off me. Please stop kissing me."

It was a plea, not a request. From her responsive lips he knew she wanted him as much as he wanted her, but the tone in her voice told him that she knew, just as he did, that their pairing wasn't right.

Slowly, gently, he disengaged his mouth from hers and let his hands fall to his sides.

Her green eyes drilled a hole straight through him

and he dropped into the luminous depths. He feared he was in jeopardy of losing his very soul.

He almost kissed her again.

And then the phone rang. The damnable, blessed telephone.

"Excuse me," he said to her, and moved to pick up the receiver. "Hello?"

"Samuel O'Neil Stevenson, do you have a woman in your house?"

"Aunt Polly."

"Don't you Aunt Polly me. Virginia Marston just called. Apparently some crazed woman climbed her fence, sprinted across her backyard and ran into your house. Are you up to your old shenanigans?"

"No, Auntie." Sam rolled his eyes to the ceiling.

"You know the road to hell is paved with S-E-X."

"I thought you wanted me to give you grandnieces and nephews." He couldn't resist the urge to tease his aunt.

"Not like that," she sputtered. "The regular way. Get married first."

"Well, I can put your mind at ease, Auntie, I'm not having sex."

At least not right now.

Sam glanced over at Edie. She was studying him like a scientist at a microscope. He pressed the receiver against his chest. "My Aunt Polly," he told her.

"Sam? Sam?" Despite being muffled by his sweat-shirt, Aunt Polly's voice rang out across the kitchen. "Did you say something to me? Are you still there?"

Letting out a long-suffering breath, Sam returned the receiver to his ear. "I'm here."

Edie silently mouthed, "I'm leaving. See you at work tomorrow."

Sam ached to tell her not to go. He wanted her to stay but at the same time he wanted her as far away as possible. Hell, he didn't know what he wanted. The woman muddled his brain, skewered his thinking, scrambled his good intentions.

"We can't have strange women climbing over fences to get to you," Aunt Polly droned in his ear.

"No, ma'am." He watched Edie turn and walk away. His gaze fixed on the hole in her pants, her round, firm buttocks peeping through and felt himself grow hard all over again.

Damn Snookems for biting her.

Damn Aunt Polly for interrupting.

But most of all, damn himself for wanting Edie Preston more than he had ever wanted any woman in his life.

IF DR. BRADDICK knew what had gone on in Sam's kitchen, he would force her to abandon the project. If he knew the feelings raging in her heart he would probably kick her out of the doctoral program all together. Edie groaned and sank lower into the tub.

What was she going to do?

Edie drained the water from the tub, got out and wrapped a towel around herself.

Her attraction to Sam threatened to ruin her dissertation project, but if she gave up her case study, what chance did she have of actually helping him and others like him?

More than anything, she needed to prove that Sam was worth saving. In order to accomplish her goal she had to keep her sexual feelings on a short leash. No matter how she might desire him, she simply could not act on those desires.

But one thing he'd said stuck in her brain and refused to let go.

How could she hope to understand her patients if she herself had never succumbed to her darker urges?

Take a walk on the wild side, he'd dared.

Sam was absolutely correct. She had no idea what it was like to let loose and really live. Despite being halfway through her Ph.D., Edie's education had been sadly lacking.

But if she did decide to broaden her horizons, it could not be with Sam.

Edie slipped into her bathrobe, ran a comb through her hair and was padding to the bedroom when the telephone rang.

Sam, she thought immediately. But why would he call her?

Snagging the cordless phone on the second ring, she perched on the edge of the bed. "Hello?"

"Edie?"

"Yes?"

"This is Jules. Jules Hardy from the department store."

"Hey, how are you?"

Jules Hardy was a busty, bubbly redhead who worked in cosmetics. Jules never lacked for dates and always had wild tales to tell about her adventures and misadventures as a young, single woman living *la vida loca* in the twenty-first century. Now if Edie ever wanted to take a walk on the wild side, this was the woman to teach her how.

"Listen, I'm in a bit of a pickle, and I heard you were studying to be a head shrinker."

"Psychologist. Yes, that's true." Edie tucked a strand of wet hair behind one ear. "What can I do for you, Jules?"

"Well, I'd rather not get into the details over the phone. It's kinda personal and involves my new boyfriend, Kyle Spencer. In fact, Kyle is the one who told me to call you."

Edie tightened her grip on the receiver. Kyle Spencer. One of the men from the halfway house she'd gone to bat for with Carmichael. She gulped. "Is Kyle in some sort of trouble?"

"Kinda. It's involved."

Letting out her breath in one long expiration, Edie lay back on the bed. "Legal trouble?"

Was Kyle mixed up in the store thefts? Was that
what worried Jules?

"I need to see you face-to-face. This is rather pri-
vate. Can we meet somewhere?"

Edie glanced at the bedside clock. Ten minutes after ten. She usually went to bed at ten-thirty. But
someone needed her. Someone was in trouble and she
could help.

"Well…"

"Oh, please," Jules said. "I really need your expertise."

"All right."

"Can you meet me at the coffee shop on Wayfarer
Lane in an hour?"

"I'll be there."

"Thank you, Edie. You're the greatest. I appreciate
this so much."

"You're welcome."

"See you then."

Jules rang off and Edie hung up the phone, wondering what in the heck she'd just committed herself
to.

SAM ARRIVED AT Carmichael's before dawn and
slipped around the back to the freight entrance as he
had every morning since starting this assignment. The
security guard went off duty at 4:00 a.m., and the
dock workers didn't arrive until six. For two hours
the inside of the store remained unguarded. If anyone

wanted to steal a big shipment of goods, this was the time to do it.

After secreting himself in the shrubbery to the left of the loading dock, he pulled a doughnut from his jacket pocket. It was a little worse for the wear, squashed flat, the chocolate glaze sticking to the waxed paper wrapping, but he was too hungry to care.

He wished for a cup of strong coffee because he hadn't gotten much sleep either, thanks to one Edie Preston.

Edie, of the impish face and infectious grin. Edie with the short, curly hair that made him think of fizzy ginger ale—light, bubbly, refreshing. Edie, who tended to stick that cute little nose of hers in where it didn't belong for all the right reasons. She cared about people. Truly cared. Sam could honestly say he'd never met anyone quite like her.

Darn the woman. Why couldn't he get her off his mind and out of his dreams?

He waited.

A battered brown Chevrolet cruised by.

Sam narrowed his eyes. It looked a lot like Harry Coomer's car. He sat up straighter. He knew that all the workers from the halfway house, Joe, Kyle and Harry, had a strict curfew. They had to stay in from midnight to 6:00 a.m. If that was Harry, then he was out of the halfway house illegally.

The car turned around at the far end of the mall parking lot and looped back. It looked a hell of a lot

like Harry's car. The vehicle slowed as it neared Carmichael's. The light from the street lamps swept over
the front of the car as it drove past, and caught the
glint of something metal swinging from the rearview
mirror.

Harry had a rabbit's foot on a metal chain dangling
from the mirror of his car.

It had to be Harry Coomer's vehicle. Whether
Harry was in it or not, Sam didn't know.

He held his breath and waited. The car looped
around the parking lot once more, then disappeared.

Time ticked by.

Fifteen minutes. Twenty. Half an hour.

The car did not return.

Sam stifled a yawn and shifted on the ground, his
buttocks growing stiff from the cold.

And speaking of buttocks, he wondered about
Edie's dog-nipped fanny.

Her compact female tush dominated his fantasies
with irritating regularity. For a few wonderful minutes
yesterday evening, he'd held that dainty fanny in his
palms.

"Knock it off, Stevenson," he growled under his
breath when his fantasizing about Edie began to cause
an unexpected stirring below his belt. He was on
stakeout for crying out loud; he could not afford this
distraction.

But he could not prevent his masculine imagination
from exploding. He saw her. In his house. On his bed.

Naked. The glory of her exposed for him alone. Her sweet lips pressed to his; her soft body held close.

Sam gulped.

Then, as if his dream had sprung to life, he saw her. Not in his mind's eye. Not in his fantasy. Not in his lingering memories.

There. In front of him. Not ten yards away from where he sat hidden in the bushes.

Edie Preston. With some big-chested, red-haired girl he recognized from Carmichael's cosmetics counter.

They were standing at the loading dock entrance, fumbling with the key code to the alarm system.

Sam rubbed his eyes. Surely, he must be seeing things. What was Edie doing here at this time of morning hanging out with a girl who possessed a questionable reputation at best? And why were they attempting to gain unauthorized entry into Carmichael's?

"OKAY," Jules said, punching in some numbers on the keypad outside the freight entrance. The heavy metal doors jerked and rolled upward with a loud clang. Edie winced against the noise and cast furtive glances over her shoulder.

"When we get inside," Jules continued, "there's another control panel on the right wall that mans the security cameras storewide. All we have to do is deactivate them, and we're free to roam about the store undetected."

"And you have the security code to that, too?"

Jules nodded.

"How did you get these codes?" Edie whispered, tip-toeing in behind Jules who had switched on a flashlight.

They found themselves standing on the loading dock surrounded by towers of boxes. Jules hit a lever mounted at the wall and the door fell closed behind them with a loud rattle.

"I used to date the manager before Mr. Trotter. Dave Highsmith. He gave me the codes so we could meet in the store after hours." Jules slanted Edie a glance.

"I'm worried that when Trotter reviews the security tapes he's going to notice the time lapse and figure out someone shut off the camera for ten or fifteen minutes," Edie said.

Jules shrugged. "It's a risk we'll have to take. He has no way of knowing it was us."

Edie shook her head. "Let's just get this over with and get out of here."

She hadn't slept a wink. She had been with Jules at the all-night diner on Wayfarer Street planning this excursion and waiting for 4:00 a.m. to roll around. Jules knew that the store's indoor security guard's shift ended two hours before the first dock worker arrived at six. After hearing Jules's story, Edie knew they had no recourse but to break into the store. Not if they wanted to keep Kyle out of jail and Jules from getting fired.

Apparently, on the previous evening, Jules had hidden in the rest room until the store closed, in order to rendezvous with Kyle, whose shift in the maintenance department ended an hour after closing time. According to Jules, they had made wild passionate love on the cosmetics counter completely unaware that a new security camera had just been added to that department in the wake of the thefts.

When he got back to the halfway house, Kyle had learned from Joe, who'd seen the invoices, about the new cameras and he'd called Jules in a panic. Since the security cameras were reviewed first thing every morning by Mr. Trotter, it was essential that someone get into the store before dawn and steal the incriminating tape.

Kyle couldn't help because he was unable to leave the halfway house after curfew. A tape of Jules and Kyle in the store alone after hours was enough to raise suspicion about their involvement in the thefts. Kyle could be sent back to jail on parole violation and Jules would be fired. And no doubt Edie would lose her job, too, since she'd laid her reputation on the line when she'd vouched for Kyle.

Edie groaned inwardly at the thought, which had been circling her head since Jules had poured out her tale of woe.

No job. No Sam. No dissertation subject.

She'd been awfully fortunate that Jules had come to her. Otherwise…Edie shuddered at the thought.

But before Edie and Jules did anything, they had to shut off all the security cameras so they wouldn't be taped sneaking into the store. With only a pencil thin beam of light to guide them, they made a beeline for the camera control panel.

Of course, if they got caught, it would mean much more than being fired.

What if her arrest got on the news? Dr. Braddick would have a cow. She envisioned her parents sitting around the television set sipping their nightly herbal tea. She could hear the reporter. ''Now, for this late-breaking story. Former Girl Scout and doctoral student breaks into Carmichael's Department Store at North Hills Mall amidst allegations of thefts. What made her do it? Details at six.''

Edie pictured herself behind bars, wearing a black-and-white striped prison uniform and cringed. She couldn't go to jail! Stripes made her look hippy.

''Jules,'' Edie whispered, struggling to keep the tremor from her voice. ''Maybe this isn't such a great idea after all. Maybe we should just go to Trotter, come clean about what happened between you and Kyle and let the chips fall where they may.''

''You don't seriously think Trotter would be that forgiving, do you? He's been looking for any excuse to can Kyle and me. And he'd love to try and pin the thefts on us."

"You're probably right about that." Edie had to agree.

"We don't have any choice. You can't back out on me now."

No, she couldn't. Edie had promised and she never broke her promises, but this still felt wrong.

"Psst." Jules had already moved through the warehouse. She waved the flashlight beam at Edie. "This way."

Before Edie could protest, Jules opened the door from the loading dock into the department store. Light spilled in, illuminating the darkness and steadying Edie's nerves somewhat. She scurried after Jules.

In a flash, Jules located the small camera mounted on the back wall, and climbed up on the counter. After fumbling with the camera for a few minutes, she ejected the tape and stuck it in her pocket.

"Got it," Jules crowed triumphantly.

Edie inhaled sharply and took a step backward.

And a cold, bony finger pointed her in the back.

Edie let out a shriek and immediately clamped a hand over her mouth.

Who was jabbing her in the lower back with an unknown object?

Freaked out beyond sensibility, she leapt to one side, her arm raised reflexively in self-defense. She swung around hard to strike the man behind her.

Except it wasn't a man.

It wasn't even human.

Edie stared owlishly as a scrawny mannequin in hot pants and a halter top—would department stores ever stop putting out summer clothes in the winter?—clattered to the floor, her head and limbs disengaging in the process.

One arm whizzed over Edie's head. A leg struck her on the thigh. The head rolled like a bowling ball down the bedding aisle and disappeared under a bed draped in a cute floral print comforter Edie had been considering buying herself for Christmas.

To Edie's ears the resulting cacophony was deafening. She cringed and waited for mall security to show up with the police in tow.

"Jules?" she whispered loudly, but her new *friend,* did not answer.

Oh crud, what now?

Then from the darkened aisle a man appeared. Edie's heart galloped and her mouth grew so dry she could not speak.

This is it, she thought. *I'm going to be arrested.*

Now, she would walk that mile in Sam's shoes. Now, she would be able to relate to him. Now, she could empathize.

She could only pray her punishment would be as lenient as his had been. Her bottom lip trembled as she struggled to ward off tears. Thrusting her hands over her head, she said, "I'll go quietly officer."

"Edie?"

Her heart leapt. It wasn't a policeman or mall security.

"Sam?"

From out of nowhere he had appeared before her like a superhero to the rescue.

Sam stepped from the shadows and she saw his dear, sweet face. He could use a shave, she noticed, a heavy five-o'clock shadow graced his jaw, but he was the most wonderful sight to ever greet her eyes.

He bent down, stuck something in the top of his boot before whispering, "Are you all right? I heard a scream and came to investigate."

"I'm fine. I just knocked over a mannequin."

"What are you doing here?" he asked.

"I was about to ask you the same thing."

Sam swallowed. Edie watched his eyes. "Um…I was driving by and saw that the freight entrance door was open a crack. Considering the thefts I figured I better see what was going on."

"Rather than call the cops?"

"I don't like talking to the cops."

"What were you doing driving by at five in the morning?" Edie asked, a sinking feeling settling deep inside her. She knew he was lying. What she did not want to face was the real reason he was in the store.

"I had a wicked case of insomnia." He winked. "After you vaulted over fences to warn me, I couldn't stop thinking about you."

She wasn't going to let him sidetrack her with that charming grin. "Weren't you worried about stumbling across the thieves?"

"What is this? Twenty questions? How am I supposed to know you're not the thief?"

She narrowed her eyes at him. "I don't owe you any explanation, but I will tell you why I'm here so you don't think I've got anything to do with the stolen merchandise." Quickly, she told him about Jules and Kyle and the ruinous security tape.

"So you two turned off the security cameras?" he asked when she finished.

"Uh-huh."

He breathed a sigh of relief. "That's good to know we're not on camera right now."

Then a sudden, horrible thought occurred to her. What if she'd been set up? What if Jules and Kyle and Sam were all in on the store thefts and they were using her as an alibi? It made perfect sense. The cameras were off. Sam was distracting her. Jules had disappeared. For all she knew Kyle had sneaked out of the halfway house. Good grief! Joe and Harry could be involved as well. At this very moment, they could be loading stolen goods into a van bound for Mexico.

Edie brought a hand to her head. How gullible was she to have fallen for Jules's story? She was too trusting, too eager to help, too darn unsuspecting.

Don't assume anything, Edie. See if you can get to the bottom of this.

"I better help you clean this up." Sam pointed at the dismantled mannequin. "The lady sorta went to pieces."

A hysterical giggle born of fear and embarrassment erupted in Edie's throat. "Poor girl lost her head."

"Flipped her wig." Sam bent and picked up a mop of fake hair.

"She doesn't have a leg to stand on." She shouldn't be laughing but she couldn't seem to help herself.

"This tragic lady reminds me of a song I wrote when I was in high school," he said picking up mannequin spare parts.

"You write songs?" Edie swallowed her laughter and ended up hiccuping.

"Not really. I only wrote this one to rebel against my Aunt Polly who forced me to join the Glee Club. She thought it would keep me out of trouble."

Edie pushed a strand of hair from her eyes and studied him in the thick shadows. There. He'd just told her something personal about himself.

Great. He picks this time and this place to bare his soul when at any moment they risked discovery.

"How does the song go?" she asked.

Sam picked up the mannequin's torso and tucked it under his arm. "Let me see if I can remember."

"I once had a robot girlfriend," Sam sang, his rich baritone voice filling the store, putting her at ease.

"With a pretty, mechanical smile. She wasn't very romantic, until I turned her dial."

He picked up the mannequin's errant leg and attached it to her body. "When I switched on her power and energized her soul, her tiny tin lips would open and her blue plastic eyes would roll. I got her at a bargain, from a strange mail-order place. She came to me disassembled and packed down in a case. I studied her schematics, then put her arms in place, wired up her circuits and bolted on her face."

Their eyes met. He grinned.

"I kept her in my closet, standing in her case," Sam crooned. "So somebody wouldn't see her and say 'Oh what a disgrace'."

He attached the other leg, then crammed the headless mannequin back on her pedestal. "But then one morning early, I found a little note, when I decoded the symbols and read what my darling wrote."

Dramatically, Sam clutched a hand to his chest. "My head then started spinning, and I with anger turned green. For my little robot girlfriend had eloped with a pinball machine."

Edie collapsed on the floor, laughing. "You're a poet," she managed to wheeze between the helpless giggles. "A true artist."

Chuckling, Sam sat down beside her, and pulled his knees to his chest. "Aunt Polly wasn't too happy when the Glee Club decided to perform 'Robot Girlfriend' at the spring recital."

Edie gazed into his eyes. He was such a fascinating, complex man. Now she knew for sure that doing a case study on him was the right thing. ''Who broke your heart?''

''Me? Who says anyone broke my heart?''

''I'm a psychologist, remember? That song is a dead giveaway. You might have thought you were composing it to irk your Aunt Polly, but whether you knew it or not, you had an ulterior motive.''

An emotion she couldn't quite identify flitted across his face and she knew he was about to deny that anyone had ever hurt him, then unexpectedly, he confessed. ''Head cheerleader, Beth Ann Pulaski. She wanted me to be something I wasn't. Clichéd story. Rich girl, poor boy from the wrong side of the tracks. In the end when she realized she couldn't make a silk purse from a sow's ear, she dumped me for the first-string quarterback.''

Edie reached out and touched his hand. ''It still hurts, doesn't it?''

He shook his head. ''Nah. I'm not that goofy kid anymore. But I did learn something from Beth Ann and I guess that's reflected in my song. Birds of a feather flock together. You can't be something you're not and there is no point in pursuing a relationship with a woman who can't accept you for yourself.''

His eyes drilled into her.

She and Serenading Sam were alone, except for the erstwhile Jules, illegally, in a department store that had been experiencing a rash of thefts, and for all she knew, he was in on it.

She wouldn't jump to conclusions. She would not. She'd made a mistake over the Corvette, assuming Sam had stolen it. She wasn't about to make a fool of herself for the second time in as many days by accusing him of being in the store for nefarious purposes.

But why else was he here? She didn't buy his insomnia story. Not for a moment. She needed to get out of here and away from him as soon as possible. She needed time to think, to decipher her confusing feelings for him.

Edie gulped. "Can you help me find the mannequin's head? When last seen it was rolling for freedom down the aisle of the bedding department."

"Ah, Marie Antoinette lives."

"You're so funny."

He reached out for her hand. "Hold on to me, I don't want you to slip and fall in the darkness."

Hesitantly, she placed her hand into his and allowed him to guide her toward the bed where the mannequin's head had disappeared.

"Which way did she go?"

"Under there." Edie pointed to the bed in question.

Sam dropped to all fours, lifted the dust ruffle and peered underneath the bed.

Edie didn't mean to take a long, lingering gander at his bottom wagging so enticingly in the air but she just couldn't help herself. She admired the way his blue jeans molded to his muscles, enjoyed the thrill that exploded in her belly.

A few minutes passed while he tried to dislodge the hapless mannequin's head. He cursed under his breath, then got to his feet.

A cobweb dangled from his hair.

"Hold still." Edie rose up on her toes and brushed the web away with her hand.

Their eyes met.

She could feel his breath on her skin.

"Thank you."

"How about the mannequin?" she asked, anxious to alter the chemistry between them before something happened.

"Wedged between the wall and the headboard. I think I can reach it from the top." He turned and climbed onto the bed.

"Let me see." Edie sat beside him and they both peered down the back of the headboard. Sure enough Marie Antoinette stared sightlessly up at them.

"What can we dislodge her with?" he mused.

"Curtain rod?"

"Excellent idea."

Edie scooted off the bed and retrieved a curtain rod from the next department. She returned, brandishing it like a sword.

"En garde," she said, feeling like she needed to do something to keep the mood light, to keep herself from dwelling on the reason why Sam had shown up out of nowhere.

"Okay, Zorro, calm down." He reached for the curtain rod. Their hands touched, kindling the growing spark between them.

Edie jerked her hand away.

Sam dropped his gaze, and resumed his position on his knees in the middle of the bed.

Neither of them commented on the power surge of emotions that resulted every time they touched.

He slipped the curtain rod behind the headboard. "It's really stuck," he said after a few moments. Using the curtain rod like a fulcrum, Sam shoved with all his strength. The head gave way, throwing him off balance.

He fell backward. Onto Edie. His large body covering hers.

Quickly, he shifted.

Edie looked up. Sam peered down.

And then he kissed her. Softly at first, then harder.

Edie's world tilted, whirled. She was lying on a bed in Carmichael's, the most incredible man in the world spread out on top of her. A man with lips of pure gold. At any moment they could be caught and arrested. Any moment they could be discovered. By kissing him here, now, in this way she was jeopardizing everything she held dear.

"We better stop this," she said, her voice shaky. What was she thinking? Hadn't she warned herself repeatedly after that incident in his kitchen that she would keep her physical distance from him? He was a man who needed the benefits of her clinical expertise. He was not, under any circumstances, a potential mate.

Sam sat up.

One of his pant legs had risen up on a shin. Edie glanced down, saw something poking from his boot.

She caught her breath, raised her head, met his eyes.

Why was the butt of a handgun protruding from the top of his boot?

7

SAM'S EYES followed Edie's gaze. He leaned over and with a quick flick of his wrist, pulled his pant leg down to conceal the gun-toting boot. Calmly, as if nothing had happened, he straightened and stared her in the face.

"Why don't you let me take you to breakfast?" he asked.

He has got a gun!

But he is not pointing it at you.

Yes, but why did he have a gun in the first place? Only policemen and criminals hid weapons in their eel-skin Justins.

And she knew he wasn't a cop. He'd told her he was working out a community service obligation.

I will not jump to conclusions. I will not jump to conclusions.

Unfortunately, the conclusions were jumping onto her. What other explanation might there be for his behavior?

"Breakfast?" he asked again.

"I can't." She waved helplessly at the cosmetics counter. "I've got to find Jules."

Sam leaned close, and whispered in her ear. "Sweetheart, it might be a good idea if you and your friend left the store."

Was he warning her off because something was about to go down? Wasn't that how criminals referred to their heists?

"Yes. That's probably a good idea. Thank you."

He just kept looking at her. Edie's stomach dove to her feet. Why did she possess such a need to help him? How had he ensnared not only her curiosity but her desire as well?

She should stay away from him for so many reasons. For the sake of her dissertation, for the sake of her job, for the sake of her sanity. Before meeting Sam Stevenson, she had never considered doing something this crazy.

He wasn't good for her.

Not at all.

He stood, retrieved the loose head and rested it back on the mannequin's body.

"Hey, Edie. Who's this?" Jules popped from behind a panty hose display. "Oh, wait a minute." She snapped her fingers. "You're Santa. Did Edie call you and tell you to meet her here or something?"

"There you are!" Edie exclaimed. "Where have you been, Jules?"

"Actually, at first I thought you'd gotten nabbed by mall security. When you screamed I dove for cover. Then I heard talking. When bedsprings started creaking, I figured you two were taking advantage of the cameras being turned off and needed your privacy.''

''It wasn't like that,'' Edie protested.

Jules smirked. ''No? Then how come he's got lipstick on his collar?''

Sam rested a hand at his collar as Edie turned to see her lipstick smeared across his white shirt. She felt embarrassed heat rise to her cheeks.

''Well, it's been nice chatting with you, Sam,'' Edie said as if they were at a cocktail party instead of locked after hours in a department store. ''But we've got to go.''

''Allow me to walk you ladies to your car,'' Sam said, then looped his arms through theirs and guided them back out the way they'd come.

''STEVENSON,'' Chief Timmons growled over the phone. ''I want some answers and I want them now.''

Bleary-eyed, Sam rolled over and stared at the clock. Seven-thirty. He'd gotten back from Carmichael's less than an hour ago. He'd thought he would catch a few hours of much needed sleep before he had to be back at the store by ten for another day of Ho, Ho, Ho.

''What's the matter?''

''I just got a call from J. D. Carmichael and he is fit to be tied.''

Sam swung his legs over the edge of the bed. "What for?"

"Last night, while you were supposedly staking out his store, over five thousand dollars worth of perfume was stolen from the cosmetics department."

Last night? Cosmetics? Sam groaned inwardly. Jules and Edie had been in the cosmetics department.

But he'd left with them. They couldn't have hidden five-thousand dollars worth of perfume on their persons.

That didn't mean they hadn't stolen the items before he had gotten into the store and hid them somewhere to be picked up later by an accomplice.

Except Edie would never steal. She was too honest and aboveboard. Too unerringly good. Besides, she was simply too smart to do something so dumb.

But he had witnessed her entering the store with his own eyes.

Could she possibly be a thief?

No way.

How well do you really know her, Stevenson? Some of the sweetest faces can hide the most treacherous hearts.

His mind balked. He could not believe that of Edie. She'd come to his house to warn him; to save him from the police. She was a reformer, a rescuer, a crusader. She didn't know the first thing about criminal offenses.

But Jules Hardy had free reign of the store while

Edie and he had been otherwise occupied. Had there been another accomplice secreted somewhere? That would explain the male voice he'd heard coming from Trotter's office. Say Jules's boyfriend, Kyle Spencer? Sam had a strong suspicion the story Jules had given Edie was false. What had really been on that security camera tape? Jules stealing perfume?

"And that's not all," Timmons continued. "When Trotter and the security team reviewed the tapes this morning they discovered that the cameras had been turned off for twenty-five minutes."

"You don't say."

"Do you know anything about that?"

"Not really," he hedged. He hadn't been the one to turn the cameras off.

"What have you got to say in your defense, Stevenson?"

"It's under control, Chief."

"Is it really? Are you aware that more items have disappeared since you started working at Carmichael's than before?"

"I promise, I've got a handle on it." Sam scratched his jaw and yawned.

"What's your next move?"

"Believe it or not I'm going to a strip club on Saturday night with the three guys I suspect might be behind the whole thing. Harry Coomer was out past curfew. I saw him driving around the mall." He also had concerns about Kyle Spencer but if he voiced those to his chief he'd be forced to explain about finding Jules and Edie in the store and he wasn't ready to come clean about that.

"This better be all business, Stevenson."

"It is. You know I'm not the strip club type." Unless it was Edie undressing herself for his eyes only.

The chief's voice changed. "I'm worried about you, Sam."

"Worried about me, sir? Whatever for?"

"This assignment was supposed to help you focus, instead you seem distracted."

"I'm not distracted," Sam denied.

"Just solve the case. And please try to wrap it up before anything else is stolen." Then the Chief hung up without saying goodbye.

Case study—Sam Stevenson
Observation—December 10

Yesterday subject was found to possess a firearm—reason unknown. Today, subject is his usual jovial self when dealing with children. Subject offered no explanation for his appearance in the store after hours on December 9. The fact that more merchandise turned up stolen during this same time frame causes this observer to wonder if the subject might have been involved.

EDIE PAUSED and stared at the wall. She was sitting in the employee lounge on her lunch break, catching up on her notations. What else could she say about Sam?

Sam remained an enigma despite having revealed a small part of himself to her when he'd sang her the robot girlfriend song.

He was kind, handsome, good-natured, understanding.

But he stole cars and he carried a gun. And maybe he was responsible for the department store thefts.

Never mind that he wrote songs about teenage heartbreak at the hands of the head cheerleader. Sam possessed a darker side that she must uncover.

She had to find out more about him. About his personal life. Who his parents were. How he'd been raised. Who was Aunt Polly?

Genetics and environment. Those clues held the keys that unlocked behavior. She would find her answers in Sam's past.

Yet how did she go about getting this information without quizzing him directly?

It wasn't as if she could get him to croon to her in the darkness again. Unless…

What better way than a date? You were supposed to reveal all that getting-to-know you stuff on a first date.

Yet did she dare get that close to him again given the fact she had very little control over her emotions when she was in his presence? Even working beside him at the store was torture. On a date he would expect more kisses. Kisses would only lead to trouble. Before she embarked on this endeavor she had to be sure she could handle any sexual overtures.

And, would Dr. Braddick approve of her dating him even if it was the only real way to obtain in-depth information?

Edie toyed with a strand of her hair, twisting it around her index finger before making up her mind. She pressed her pen to the paper.

Problem—obtaining information without appearing obvious.

Solution—meet subject in a casual social situation.

Plan of action—ask subject out on a date.

THREE DAYS LATER, on Saturday afternoon, she finally worked up the courage to ask Sam out. Her palms were so sweaty she had to wipe them against her pant legs. She'd never asked out a guy before. It was more difficult than she thought it would be.

Throughout the day, she'd cast furtive glances his way. He looked so jovial in that Santa suit, smiling and joking with the children, but Edie knew what lay beyond the padding and the fake beard. Yards and yards of lean, muscular male. Even now, watching him give the last child in line a candy cane, tingles bubbled inside of her.

Santa, you can come down my chimney any time.

Immediately she mentally chastised herself for that dangerous thought. Much as she might like getting close to Santa on a physical level, she could not. This relationship must remain strictly aboveboard. No more stolen kisses. No more lying underneath him on Carmichael's bedding. No more late-night fantasies about what might have been.

Sam met her gaze, his eyes twinkling mischievously as if he could read her mind. "Ready to call it a night?" He stepped down from the sleigh and turned to leave.

Edie gulped. "Sam."

He stopped and favored her with a grin worth committing a carnal sin for.

"What is it, Edie?"

"I was wondering..." She couldn't even look him in the eye. Edie stared intently at her hands. This would be easier if he wasn't wearing a red suit and artificial whiskers.

"Yes?" His voice was soft, enticing.

Just say the words, Edie.

"I was wondering, if you're not busy, would you like to go out tonight?"

He crooked a finger under her chin, raised her face to meet his. "I'd like that very much, but I'm afraid I've got plans tonight."

"Plans?" she repeated like an idiot.

"I'm going out with Joe and Kyle and Harry. We've had this planned for two weeks and...."

"That's okay." She pulled away from him, her heart sinking into her shoes with disappointment. He was spending his evening with the guys. Not even a date with her could cancel his plans. What did that mean? Would Sam rather be with them than with her? "No problem."

"But I'd be happy to go out with you tomorrow night."

"Really?" Her pulse leapt joyously. Was she pathetic or what?

"Sure. You can pick me up at eight."

"Great." Edie smiled and watched him walk away.

Then it dawned on her. He was going out with the three worst guys in the world for him to be with.

Where were they going? Edie thought about the store thefts. Might they be involved? All four of them in on it together, maybe even Jules, too? She grimaced. She hated to believe the worst about any of them but the facts were staring her in the face. Sam in the store without reasonable explanation. Joe was good with money. Kyle knew the store security codes. Harry had underworld connections. Were they planning on fencing the items or whatever it was that thieves did with stolen merchandise?

She had to know for sure if Sam was involved in the department store thefts. She had to put her mind at ease once and for all. Like it or not, she had to follow him again.

THE FOUR OF THEM crowded into Joe's compact car and headed for the strip club masquerading under the guise of a gentleman's cabaret.

Harry talked nonstop about how his sexy girlfriend was going to wow their pants off. Sam couldn't help thinking that no matter how well put together the woman might be, she couldn't hold a candle to a certain little elf. An elf that had taken up permanent residence in his head.

Sam couldn't stop thinking about Edie and their impending date. This wasn't good. This wasn't right. He should be concentrating on the job at hand. He should be finding out if the men in the car with him were stealing from Carmichael's Department Store. What he should not be doing was pining over a woman who wanted nothing more than to reform him. To mold him into the man she yearned for him to be.

Wincing inwardly, he recalled the early-morning hours on that bed in Carmichael's Department Store with Edie's hot little body crushed beneath his. Even now his lower region tightened with the memory of her wriggling beneath him.

He had been out of his ever loving mind telling her about Beth Ann Pulaski and singing her the robot girlfriend song. Why had he revealed so much about himself to her?

A weak moment. It was his only excuse. His sudden loquaciousness had nothing to do with her delicious scent or her wide green eyes or the way her little giggle thrilled him to the bone.

Why couldn't he stop thinking about the taste of those sweet red lips, the feel of her satin soft skin, the sound of her breathy voice?

No woman had ever dominated his wakefulness like this. Not even Beth Ann and he'd been a randy teenager at the time.

Edie.

Innocent and feisty. Determined and loyal. Caring and kind and considerate.

She had no place in his life, nor he in hers.

But he wanted her.

With a fierceness that scared him.

When had he become so vulnerable to her charms? How had he allowed this to happen?

Sam was so busy berating himself he hadn't realized they'd pulled into the club parking lot until Joe shut off the engine.

Neon lights flashed—Girls, Girls, Girls. On top of the building was a lighted caricature of a voluptuous female wriggling out of her G-string. The bump and grind music from inside the building throbbed so loudly they could feel the vibrations through the floorboard of the car.

''Ready boys?'' Joe asked.

Harry and Kyle cheered. Sam forced a noise of enthusiasm.

Okay, he told himself. *Get on the ball. The sooner*

you solve the case the sooner you can quit being Santa.

And the sooner he could get away from Edie Preston and her bewitching spell.

8

THEY WERE GOING to a strip bar! Edie watched from the parking lot of Sinbad's Gentlemen's Cabaret as Joe, Harry, Kyle and Sam walked in the front door.

She sighed. Men.

For Harry, Kyle and Joe, she knew the temptation to drink would be strong. For Sam, Edie wasn't sure what would tempt him the most. Drink or naked feminine flesh.

Did she really want to find out?

The words Sam had spoken to her in his house the day she'd suspected him of stealing the Corvette rattled in her head.

Before you're ever going to relate to your patients, before you can ever really understand people, you're going to have to take a walk on the wild side.

Yes. She wanted to know. What was it about the wild side that so gripped Sam?

She parked in a far corner of the lot and sat there a few minutes collecting her courage. She could do this. All in the name of science. This was for her dissertation. Nothing personal. Right?

Taking a deep breath, Edie got out of the car. Rain

had fallen earlier in the day and cool humidity permeated the night air. She pulled the collar of her coat tightly around her neck and eased up to the door.

The sound of Donna Summer's "Hot Stuff" blasted.

Edie slipped inside and stood in the darkness of the entry way, taking in the sights before her.

Three near-naked women danced and twirled on a stage in the center of the room while a fog machine occasionally belched out clouds of smoke. Strobe lights gyrated.

The place was so dark Edie could barely see in front of her. She inched forward, and took an empty chair at a table in the back.

She hadn't located Sam and his friends. She slipped from her coat, removed her mittens and rubbed her palms together.

"What'll ya have?" A waitress with a Pamela Anderson figure wearing a barely there outfit fashioned after a tuxedo, hovered near Edie's elbow.

"I'm fine thanks." Edie smiled.

"There's a two-drink minimum," the waitress had to shout to be heard above the noise.

"Oh, well, in that case I'll have a cola."

"It'll cost you seven-fifty."

"Seven dollars and fifty cents!"

"Or you could get an alcoholic beverage for the same price," the woman suggested with a shrug.

Edie had never consumed alcohol before but it seemed extravagant to pay seven-fifty for a cola.

Take a walk on the wild side.

"Okay," she said. "I'll have a drink."

The waitress looked at her expectantly.

"You want to know what kind of drink?" Edie asked.

"That'd be a start."

"Uh, well, what do you suggest?"

"Beer, wine, mixed drink. Mixed drink's are the best bargain for the money."

"All right then, I'll have a mixed drink." Edie folded her hands together on the table.

The waitress sighed. "What kind of mixed drink?"

"You choose."

"How about a Slow Comfortable Screw?"

"Beg pardon?"

Was the woman suggesting some sort of kinky sexual proposition? Fear clinched her stomach. She was in way over her head.

"Don't panic honey." The woman laid a hand on her shoulder. "I don't want to take you to bed. A Slow Comfortable Screw is a drink."

Edie felt her face flame in the darkness. She wanted the woman to leave as quickly as possible. "Yes, bring me two of those comfortable thingies."

"Why do I get the feeling I'm not going to get a tip out of this one?" the woman muttered under her breath and sashayed away, hips swinging like a pendulum.

Embarrassed at her ignorance, Edie plucked a twenty from her purse and left it on the table. She'd show that waitress that she indeed knew how to tip.

The music changed. Now they were playing "Bad Girls."

Edie studied the men sitting around the stage. They were whistling and clapping and waving bills at the women. The dancers would come over and shake their groove things in the guys' faces and relieve them of their money.

What did it feel like, Edie wondered, to strut your stuff like that? Capitalizing on men's desires to see women naked. It sounded frightening and exhilarating and bizarre.

The women strutted and flaunted their bodies. One swung around a pole as if she were a world-class gymnast. Another did the splits. A third did very strange things with a banana.

Oh, dear!

The waitress brought her drinks, whisked up the twenty and pranced over to a table full of rowdy men in cowboy hats.

Edie took a sip of her drink.

Sweet. Fruity. And it warmed her straight to her toes.

Nice. Very nice.

She took another sip and finally spotted Sam. He

and the other fellows were sitting at a table not far from the stage. Sam had his back to her, his attention riveted on the dancers.

Sadness washed over her.

Was this what he found attractive? Blatant exhibitionism? Naked female flesh swinging and twisting and cavorting under colored lights?

Apparently so.

Humph.

Edie took the thin red cocktail straw in her teeth and sucked hard.

Gosh this thing tasted good.

She fished out the cherry and chewed on it. What was that saying Jules had related to her? If you could tie a cherry stem with your tongue that meant you were good in bed.

After she swallowed the cherry, Edie sat nibbling on the stem, her gaze welded on Sam and company. He was laughing at something Joe had said.

Ha. Ha.

Still giving the cherry stem hell with her teeth, Edie took a notepad and pen from her purse. She squinted in the almost nonexistent lighting.

Case Study—Sam Stevenson
Observation—December 14

Subject has entered a strip club with three male co-workers. He seems very entertained by the more basic aspect of the male-female relationship. The stripper offers him a look at her body. He deposits money into her skimpy garter.

Edie watched Sam do just that, and she experienced a sudden urge to cry. What in the heck was the matter with her? She was simply observing him for her dissertation. She shouldn't care if he chose to visit Hugh Heffner at the Playboy Mansion. She was a scientist. A professional. Her emotions had no place in the case study.

She slammed the notebook closed, jammed it in her purse and sat trying to do the impossible—tie that silly cherry stem into a knot with her tongue.

Minutes later Edie realized she would never be good in bed. The mutilated stem fell to pieces in her mouth. She spit the shreds into a napkin and took a big swallow of her drink.

This time a warm fluffy cloud enveloped her body. Her head swam muzzily and she had the strongest urge to sing. Who invented this drink? It was wonderful.

The dancers were hoofing it to ''You Sexy Thing,'' when Edie realized she had to go to the bathroom. She pushed back her chair. The wooden legs screeched against the floor.

''Shh.'' Edie put a finger to her lips and rose to her feet.

Whoa! Why did her knees feel like overcooked noodles?

Was she tipsy?

Edie giggled. This wasn't so bad.

Now, where was the potty?

She managed to find the bathroom and on her way back to her table, she bumped into a tall, burly man with arms that bulged around the sleeves of his tight black T-shirt. He looked as if he spent a lot of time at the gym. He had been pacing in front of the door, something lacy and very skimpy clutched in his hands.

"There you are!" he said, when she jostled his elbow.

"Oops. I'm sorry."

"Okay, so you're late. Don't worry about. Just get dressed. Your set starts in seven minutes." He thrust the lacy thing at her. "And put on some more makeup."

"Makeup?"

He narrowed his eyes at her. "Mac sent you, right? Vera called in sick and Mac was suppose to send someone over."

And then it hit Edie what this man was saying. He thought she was a relief stripper come to fill in for his ailing dancer.

A wicked little voice whispered inside her head. *Take a walk on the wild side.*

She could go up on stage and dance. She could find out firsthand what it was like. It would be a perfect sidebar to her case study on Sam. She would explore his world, analyze it and use her analysis to draw conclusions about him.

She could have men ogling her and wanting to take her home.

She could have Sam's undivided attention.

The last thought cinched it.

"Yeah," Edie said. "Mac sent me."

The guy raked his gaze over her. "Mac's got good taste, I'll say that for him."

"Thank you." Edie fluttered her eyelashes at the guy, feeling more sexy and seductive than she'd ever felt in her life. It didn't hurt that she was fueled by a Slow Comfortable Screw. "Where do I change?"

The guy pointed to a door. "Through there."

"Thanks."

Pulse quick and thready with excitement, knees weak, Edie pushed through the door. She could do this. She would do this. Then Sam couldn't say she'd never done anything bad. She'd gotten drunk and now she was going to perform a striptease.

She found the dressing room easily enough. A blonde and a redhead sat in bathrobes applying a fresh round of makeup, a third woman lounged in a bean-bag chair leafing through a copy of *Real Confessions* magazine.

"Hi," Edie greeted them. "I'm new."

"Good for you," the one in the beanbag chair said without looking up.

"Mac sent me," Edie explained.

"You better quit gabbing and get dressed," the blonde at the mirror said. "You're on in five minutes."

"Oh, okay." Edie shrugged out of her coat and hung it on a rack.

"Come on, honey," the redhead said, "move it."

Hands trembling, Edie took off her clothes and slipped into the tiny outfit. A glittery gold G-string and a gauzy see-through bra.

I can't go on stage dressed like this.

But before she could back out, the redhead pushed her into a chair. "Here, I'll help you with your makeup, but just this once."

"Th-thank you," Edie stammered.

The woman slathered her in so much mascara and eyeshadow Edie feared she'd come off looking like a circus clown. But when she looked into the mirror she couldn't believe the creature that peered back.

She looked exotic, worldly and very desirable.

Her fears evaporated. She was going out there and she was going to dance for no one but Sam.

A statuesque brunette appeared from behind a curtain, perspiring and wiping her face with a towel. She turned to Edie. "You're on."

"Wait," the redhead said, slipping off her own six-inch heels and tossing them to Edie. "You'll need these."

Edie slipped on the heels and teetered before the

curtain. She took a deep breath and sucked in her tummy.

"Go on." The redhead shoved her through the curtain and Edie found herself on stage with two other women.

And she simply stood there.

"Brick House" blasted from the stereo system.

"Hey, baby," some guy from the audience leered. "Shake it!"

The stage lights blinded her. She couldn't see the audience but she could hear them out there— breathing.

Her courage slipped and she almost turned and ran.

And then she remembered Sam.

Slowly, Edie began to rotate her hips.

Sam's watching. Show him what you've got, her *inner self urged. Show him you can strip with the best of them.*

Then for his benefit alone, she danced.

EDIE?

Thunderstruck, Sam's mouth dropped open.

It couldn't be.

He rubbed his eyes with both fists. That woman had been on his mind so much he was imagining she was up there dancing on the stage for him in the most incredible little getup ever created.

Blinking, he looked again.

She was coming closer, moving gracefully as a

swan, arching her back, circling her hips, giving him a come-hither smile.

It *was* Edie!

But how? Why?

For a second, he sat frozen, stunned by her mesmerizing beauty and her unexpected act.

Then he realized that every lecherous eye in the place was trailing down her fine, firm body and a surge of hot, red jealousy shot through him.

In an instant, he was on his feet, pulling his coat from the back of his chair and heading straight toward her.

SAM WAS COMING AT HER, a grimly determined expression on his face—his jaw set, his blue eyes blazing fire.

Edie squealed and backed up.

He didn't look happy. Not a bit.

In one long-legged stride he stepped on the bottom of an empty chair next to the stage, then onto the tabletop and from there, onto the stage itself.

"Come here," he commanded.

Edie raised her palms. "What are you doing?"

"No woman of mine is going to parade herself naked in front of a bunch of slobbering strangers."

"I'm not your woman," she declared, planting her hands on her hips and staring him in the eyes. She stood up to him, defied his high-handedness, but her heart was pit-patting like the revved-up rhythm section of a world-class band. She had inspired this macho performance in him.

And he'd said that she was his woman.

Why should that make her feel so warm and happy and terribly afraid she was going to screw things up?

Customers were booing, yelling at Sam to get off the stage. From the corner of her eye Edie saw a man approaching from the back of the darkened room.

Sam stalked after her like John Wayne pursuing Maureen O'Hara in *McClintock!*.

Edie turned to run.

But the six-inch heels were her undoing. She misstepped and teetered precariously at the edge of the stage.

"Gotcha," Sam said, snaking an arm around her waist and throwing his coat over her body.

His breath was warm against her cheek, his lips oh so close, his brow pulled together in a deep, disapproving frown.

He looked mad enough to take her over his knee and spank her bare bottom.

Damn her for being thrilled about that.

Instead of spanking her, however, he picked her up as if she were no heavier than whipped cream and tossed her over his shoulder.

"Put me down," she insisted. She wasn't into this Neanderthal, me-Tarzan-you-Jane scenario. She was a modern, independent—if somewhat sheltered—

woman and if she chose to dance at a strip club that was none of Sam Stevenson's business.

Apparently, however, he was making her his business.

Edie squirmed against his shoulder, but he held her firmly in place with one hand pressed to her back.

The crowd, from her upside-down vantage point, looked weird. Their faces a mix of displeasure and laughter. Male voices whooped and hollered and then another man hopped up on the stage and went after another dancer.

Chaos ensued.

Men shouted. Tables tipped. Glass shattered. Women screamed.

"Call the cops," someone yelled.

Never missing a step, Sam calmly carried her off the stage.

Only to find his passage blocked by the burly man who'd mistaken Edie for a stripper. He had his hands folded over his massive chest.

Edie peered around Sam's shoulder. Uh-oh. The guy—who resembled a large chunk of granite—looked really mad.

"Put her down," the burly man insisted.

"Out of my way, buddy," Sam growled.

"Look what you caused." Granite-chunk swept a hand at the discord around them. "You can't touch the strippers."

"She is not a stripper," Sam said. "She's my girl-friend."

First she was his woman and now she was his girl-friend. Hmm. If she kept upgrading at this rate the next thing she knew she'd be his wife.

And unfortunately, that wasn't an entirely unpleas-ant thought.

"Put her down. I don't want to have to tell you again." Granite-chunk moved closer.

"Get out of my way," Sam said. "I'm taking her home."

Edie was getting nervous, with her fanny sticking in the air, these two massive men standing nose to nose, within seconds of duking it out.

Holding her as he was, Sam was at a disadvantage. When he tried to sidestep around Granite-chunk, the guy doubled up a powerful fist and punched Sam sol-idly in the eye.

Sam's head shot back. His knees wobbled. Edie gasped.

He let her slip to her feet.

Edie turned on Granite-chunk. "You big bully! You didn't have to hit him."

"Hey," Granite-chunk said. "Don't start with me. I was only doing my job."

Swaying slightly, Sam placed a hand to his eye, which was swelling rapidly.

"Don't just stand there," Edie snapped at Granite-chunk. "Get me an ice pack."

Dumbfounded, the guy blinked at her.

"Go on."

He moved away.

Edie turned her attention to Sam. She pulled up a nearby chair. "Sit."

He shook his head. "Not until you put on my coat."

The coat he'd wrapped her in when he'd carted her off the stage had fallen to the floor.

"Okay." Edie shrugged into the coat. It smelled of him. Musky. Male. Nice. "Now, sit down."

He obeyed.

The music had stopped and the shouting had started to die down, but Edie didn't notice.

Tenderly, she touched his eye. "You're going to have quite a shiner."

"That hurts," he complained.

"Ah, poor baby."

Sam glared at her. "Hey, I'm the one who rescued you."

"I never asked you to save me. I'm not some helpless damsel."

"Why is that, Edie? Because you're the only one who can rescue people? What's the deal, don't *you* ever need anything from anyone?"

"Hush," she admonished.

Joe Dawson came over to them. "Wow, Sam. That was so cool the way you went up on stage and dragged Edie off."

She lasered a chilly gaze at him. "Don't encourage this sort of behavior, Joe."

"When did you start dancing, Edie? If I'd known you did this on the side I would have come in here a long time ago." Joe wriggled his eyebrows.

"Shut up, Joe. Before you're sporting a shiner to match this one," Sam growled.

In the distance they heard sirens. The police were on their way.

"Maybe you and Kyle and Harry should get out of here," she suggested to Joe.

"You're probably right. But how will Sam get home?"

"I'll drive him."

One eyebrow went up on Joe's forehead. "You sure?"

"I'll be fine," Sam said.

Joe raised a hand. "Okay then, see you tomorrow, caveman."

Edie rolled her eyes.

Then, to her surprise Granite-chunk appeared with an ice pack. She thanked him nicely and pressed the pack to Sam's eye.

"We better get out of here too," he said.

"No, we'll just explain to the cops what happened."

"I don't really want to talk to the cops." He shook his head.

Right. Sam had secrets she knew nothing about.

"Let's go out the back way," he suggested.

"Yes, I need to pick up my clothes and purse."

Edie took his hand and led Sam through the back entrance. The club patrons had already cleared out considerably, leaving a huge mess behind. Once in the dressing room, Edie was dismayed to find a man and a woman locked in a passionate embrace on top of her clothes.

"Oh, excuse me," she said.

They ignored her completely.

She cleared her throat. How was she going to get her clothes out from under them?

The sirens wailed louder, sounding as if they were almost in the parking lot.

"No time to waste." Sam said, and scooped her into his arms.

"What are you doing?"

"You can't walk in those damned shoes."

"But what about my things?"

"We'll worry about that later." He carried her out the back door, Edie trying to keep the ice pack pressed to his eye.

He staggered into the parking lot.

"I'll drive us," she said.

"No way, sweetheart. That's alcohol I smell on your breath."

"I only had one Slow Comfortable Screw," she protested.

"Oh, so that's what got into you." He grinned and

despite his battered eye, or maybe because of it, he looked damned sexy. Was this guy rugged or what?

"I don't even feel tipsy any more. I can drive," she insisted.

"Hush. I'm assuming your driver's license is in your purse back there in the dressing room, so you're not even legal in that respect."

She looked up into those blue eyes and felt the pull of something inexplicable inside her. How could a man who cared enough not to let her drive while inebriated be a bad guy? Still, he seemed desperate to avoid law enforcement authorities. Why? She didn't really want to know the answer.

What did that mean? Would she ever understand him?

"I see a taxi," Sam said. "Wave your hand and flag him down."

He stepped out into the street carrying Edie, at the same time two patrol cars screeched to a stop in the club parking lot. He whistled loudly at the cab driving slowly down the street. Edie frantically waved her hand.

The taxi pulled over and they tumbled into the back seat at the same moment the police stormed into the strip club.

"Whew." Sam breathed, lolling his head against the back seat of the cab and closing his eyes. "That was a close call."

"Where to?" the taxi driver asked.

Edie leaned forward and gave the man Sam's address.

Sam opened his good eye and stared at her. "We're going to my house?"

"Yes," she said. "Someone has to tend that eye of yours."

9

THEY WERE GOING to his house.

Edie and he.

Together.

Alone.

She in that devastatingly skimpy outfit, covered only by his overcoat.

Sam swallowed a groan. He didn't think he could take much more of this.

He wanted her.

With a rampant fierceness that scared him.

She settled against the seat and glanced over at him. "Put the ice pack back on your eye."

"It's cold."

"Are you always so whiny?"

"Only when I think it will get me attention." He gave her his most endearing grin.

She wasn't impressed. "Ice. On your eye. Now. Before it blows up as big as the Goodyear Blimp."

"Yes'm. Anybody ever tell you that you're sexy when you're giving orders."

"Ice pack," she threatened.

"Okay, okay."

He pressed the heavy pack to his tender eye. Ouch. He didn't know whether his muzziness was due to the warmth of the cab's heater or the comfort of Edie's nearness but leaning back with his eyes closed, Sam must have fallen asleep. It seemed as if mere seconds later the cab pulled to a stop outside his house and Edie was nudging him with an elbow.

"Pay the man, Sam. All my money is in my purse back at the strip club."

"Oh, yeah." He shook his head and the ice pack plopped wetly into his lap. "Sure."

He fumbled in his wallet, paid the driver then got out with Edie.

"Where's your house key?" She stood on his front sidewalk, shivering in the damp night air. He wanted to put his arms around her, hold her close, warm her up.

He removed the key from his pocket and handed it over to her.

She trotted up the steps ahead of him, her sky-scraper high heels striking the cement with a provocative *click-clack* noise. Even in his damaged state Sam couldn't help admiring her legs in those danger-ous shoes. Her gams went up and up and up until they disappeared beneath the hem of his coat.

Damn, but she looked gorgeous wearing his clothes.

He would love to see her in one of his long-sleeved, white dress shirts. Or a pair of his silk boxer shorts. Or his cowboy hat and nothing else at all.

Unlocking the door she pushed it open, then stepped over the threshold and flicked on the light. She stood illuminated in the doorway like some otherworldly sprite, crooking a provocative finger at him.

"Come in where it's warm."

He obeyed, following her inside and kicking the door closed with his foot, his heart hammering so hard he feared it might spring from his chest.

Physical desire for her crashed over him in an unstoppable tidal wave. He couldn't take his eyes from her. He admired the way her bottom swished beneath the stiff fabric of his coat, envisioned the sweet, naked body beneath.

Soft curving breasts. A tiny high waist. Hips that sloped like gently rolling hills.

Mama mia! He needed hosing down with a fire extinguisher.

Every sexual fantasy he'd ever had about a woman was rolled up into this one compact, exquisite little package. And it seemed as if he'd been waiting for her his entire life.

WITH TREMBLING HANDS, Edie washed up in Sam's bathroom sink. Raising her head, she peered at herself in the mirror and catalogued her features.

Wide green eyes made even larger by an overuse of mascara, mussed amber hair, lips painted the most blatant color of scarlet, cheeks shaded with excess rouge.

A real hottie.

A fox.

A babe.

Nouns she'd never applied to herself. She didn't recognize this woman.

The lady in the mirror was a sexy siren. The type men did crazy things for—like marching onto a stage and slinging her over their shoulders. This woman was a naughty femme fatale.

Where was good girl, Edie Preston?

She looked down at Sam's coat and the towel in her hand. For the first time in her life, she felt confused about her identity.

Shaking off the sensation, Edie dried her hands and stepped from the bathroom. She had to get out of here as soon as she could. She was having some very unprofessional thoughts about Sam and if she lingered she feared what might happen between them. She'd stay just long enough to make sure that he was going to be all right and then she'd call another taxi.

She found Sam where she'd left him, sitting on the living room couch, the ice pack clutched to his right eye. She sat beside him, reached up and removed the ice pack. The room seemed very small and intimate. She had never been so aware of proximity to another human being.

"I'm sorry," she said.

"For what?"

"Causing this."

He shook his head. "You didn't cause anything."

"Just the blackening of your eye and the destruction of a bar."

"May I ask you a question?"

She shrugged. "Sure."

"What were you doing at the club tonight?"

Edie didn't answer.

"You were following me again, weren't you?"

"Yes," she admitted.

"Why?"

"I was worried about you. Hanging out with Joe and Kyle and Harry. They've all three been in prison. I know they're trying to turn their lives around, and I'm struggling not to be judgmental. But a strip club is hardly the place to start. I'm sure you're aware that by simply being in that place they were violating their parole. I'd hate to see you get involved in something unsavory."

He opened his eyes and stared up at her. His gaze so intent it robbed her of breath. "You really care what happens to me?"

"Yes," she whispered.

"Why were you up on that stage?"

"I wanted to see what it was like to take a walk on the wild side. You were right. Tonight I discovered I really haven't lived."

He reached up and wrapped a hand around her

wrist. Instantly, her pulse quickened. "No, Edie, I was wrong. You don't have to get into trouble yourself in order to be a good psychologist."

Sam swallowed hard, his Adam's apple bobbing. When he spoke again his voice was husky. "When I saw you on that stage, taking off your clothes for those barbaric guys, I lost it."

"I wasn't taking my clothes off for those men. I was taking my clothes off for you. I sat in the audience for a while, watching you watch those other women and I got jealous. Then when the guy that punched you in the eye mistook me for a stripper, I decided to go along with it."

"You were taking your clothes off for me?" He smiled.

"Duh!"

"But why?"

"Because I wanted you to want me."

"I do want you, Edie." He reached over and took her hand. "What I can't figure out is, do you want me because I represent a project for you or do you want the real me? Warts and all."

Guilt zinged through Edie. What would he think if he knew she was doing a case study on him?

His face glistening in the lamplight, hovered so close to hers.

His strong hands spanned her waist and he pulled her into his lap. "I've been fighting my desire for you," he whispered. "I know it's wrong. You deserve someone better. Someone college educated who can give you the moon.''

''You're as good as any man alive, Sam Stevenson, don't let anyone tell you otherwise. And I don't want the moon.''

''What do you want?'' His breath smelled like peppermint and his eyes shone with a fevered gleam.

At his question, a profound heat built between her legs, a heat so vehement she lost all words for speech.

''Do you want me to kiss you?''

''I can't.'' She shook her head.

''Can't or won't?''

''Shouldn't.''

''Then why did you come back here with me tonight?''

''To make sure you were going to be okay.''

''Is that the only reason?'' He tilted his head and brushed his lips lightly against the nape of her neck.

Edie moaned low in her throat. A low guttural sound she couldn't believe she had uttered.

Oh, how she wanted him.

Wanting him wasn't smart or rational. Not only was he a co-worker, and possibly a thief, but he was her dissertation project. Dr. Braddick had warned her about getting involved with him on a personal level.

But common sense didn't figure in where passion was concern. The novelty of her emotions made Edie desperate to explore him while at the same time afraid of moving forward.

Sam sensed her dilemma. "We don't have to do anything you don't want to do, sweetheart."

Sweetheart.

She loved the way he said that word. His soft intonation made her feel special in a way no man ever had. She had never allowed anyone to get this close to her before. She'd always been too busy with her studies and her efforts to help others. For many years her own needs had been put on the back burner. Now, she was blindsided by the depth of her desire.

She wanted him to make love to her. So very much.

But she could not.

Sam began to nibble on her earlobe, right and wrong muddled into a beguiling stew of hungry, aching need.

When Sam ran his tongue against the underside of her chin, caution leapt out the window leaving her shaken to the core. She didn't care about her dissertation or her job. Tomorrow loomed far in the hazy distance.

What mattered was now.

Sam's arms tightened around her and his fingers began to explore, unbuttoning the coat and running his rough callused fingers over her smooth silky skin.

He seemed to know exactly where to touch—stroking and rubbing, licking and caressing. The living room spilled into a kaleidoscope of sensation—the sight of his Christmas tree in the corner, lights merrily winking. The feel of the leather couch beneath them, the scent of Sam's hair, the taste of sin in her mouth.

With him, she danced on the wild side. Excited and exciting. Letting loose. Letting herself go free. Letting the flow take her into uncharted territory.

His coat fell away from her shoulders. His teeth nipped lightly at her exposed flesh. He buried his face in her hair and inhaled sharply.

"You smell so good," he murmured softly. "Like a Christmas angel."

His hands were at her breasts, covered only by the gauzy thin strip of material she'd worn while dancing onstage. He flicked the material out of the way with his thumbs, then bent his head to draw one perky nipple into his mouth.

His tongue was liquid fire. She writhed beneath him.

He raised his head. Their eyes met, melding into something deep and ancient.

His mouth captured hers stealing all her senses. Shivering, Edie surrendered to temptation.

HE TOOK HER to the living room rug, laid her down and gazed upon her with marvel in his heart.

The gauzy material around her breasts clung wetly to her nipples where he had just suckled. Her skin glowed in the sparkling of Christmas tree lights.

Sam caught his breath. She was so beautiful that he ached whenever he looked at her.

He held her, caressed her, kissed her. She was the rarest treasure and he wanted their first lovemaking to last a long luxurious time.

Edie came alive beneath his fingers. Her responsiveness stirred him. Her little moans sent shafts of pure desire lancing through him.

He drowned in the scent of her, exalted in her womanhood. She was the most incredible creature he'd ever met.

"Open your eyes, Edie," he murmured in her ear. "Open your eyes and see what you're doing to me."

Her eyes flew open then, and widened with wonder.

Slowly, gently, he touched her between her legs, working her to a fevered pitch.

She arched her back, called his name repeatedly.

"Do you want me, Edie? Do you want the real me, faults and all? I'm not an enchanted frog waiting for your kiss in order to turn into a prince. I can't be changed, or healed by your love," he whispered into her ear. "But tell me it doesn't matter. Tell me that you want me and me alone. Tell me that I'm enough for you."

Edie stopped moving. He propped himself up on his elbow and peered down at her. A serious expression eclipsed her previous pleasure.

"Sam." She reached a hand for him but he shied from her touch.

"You can't promise me those things, can you?" A heavy sensation dropped into his gut. She couldn't promise to take him as he was because she was just like Donna. She wanted him to be something he wasn't. She couldn't love him for himself.

"It's not that, Sam." She sat up, pushed a mop of curls from her eyes.

"What is it then?"

She snagged her bottom lip between her teeth. "I can't…there's something…it's just that I don't know the real Sam Stevenson."

"No." He had to acknowledge the truth. "You don't." How could he expect her to give him the answer he so badly needed to hear when she suspected he was a petty criminal serving out a community service sentence?

"But you could talk to me." She placed a hand on his shoulder. "You could tell me all about yourself."

He wasn't some puzzle for her to piece together. Nor was he an outlaw to be reformed, but a flesh-and-blood man with both strengths and weaknesses.

But he could not tell her these things. Because of his job, he'd been forced to lie. About himself. About his motives. This was wrong. No matter how right it might feel.

He shook his head, draped his elbow across his knee. "Maybe it would be best if you went home."

She stared at him a moment, then drew in a long breath. "Perhaps you're right."

"Just because we have this animal magnetism going on between us doesn't mean we have to act on it.''

She nodded. ''Exactly.''

He got to his feet, held out a hand to her. ''I'll call you a cab.''

EDIE STARED OUT the rear window as the taxi pulled away from Sam's house, her heart wrenching in emotional pain, her body still aching with suppressed need.

He stood bare-chested in the doorway, waving goodbye, a sad expression on his face. Edie watched until the car went around the corner, then she turned to face forward.

She pulled his coat tightly around her shoulders, brought the collar to her nose, inhaled the scent of him and very quietly started to cry.

She shouldn't have been so disappointed in the way things had turned out, but she was. Miraculously, Sam had saved her from making a terrible mistake, rather than taking advantage of her during a vulnerable moment. If she had made love to him she would not only have irrevocably ruined her dissertation but she would have lost her power to help Sam.

For in her heart Edie knew that if they had consummated their simmering attraction, she would have lost what shred of objectivity she had left.

She would have lost her head as well as her heart.

It was better this way.

Much better.

She had chosen the correct course. She'd done what was expected of her. She had been a good girl. She hadn't completely sacrificed her dissertation. She'd done the right thing.

If that was true, why did she feel so empty inside?

Nothing made sense anymore. Not her education or her job. Not her need to help others.

The only thing in her life that made sense was back there in that house on Sylvan Street. The one thing that she could not have.

10

HE HAD FALLEN in love with her. That realization shook Sam to his very essence.

A week had passed since they had almost made love at his house. A week filled with tortured thoughts and sleepless nights. A week of struggling to focus on his job with miserable results.

He could not stop thinking about her, no matter how hard he tried.

When he sat in his kitchen, he could see her bent over the table, her fanny in the air, her blue jeans ripped. When he went to the drugstore to pick up prescriptions for Aunt Polly, he saw her sprawled out on the floor covered in condoms. When he sat on the couch and pressed the sofa pillows to his nose, he could smell her sweet lovely scent.

And at work, his eyes followed around the room like a lost puppy dog.

Somewhere, somehow, despite his best intentions to the contrary, he'd fallen for her.

Did he dare trust his feelings? He thought he'd been in love before but Donna had only loved him when he did what she wanted.

Being in love again was the last thing he wanted.

Especially with Edie. They were an impossible match. The bad boy and the crusader. The cynic and Miss Merry Sunshine.

Except he wasn't all that bad any more and hadn't been for a long time. Not counting blowing up the mayor's Lexus.

But too many women had tried to change him in the past, seeking to mold him into the image they wanted. First Aunt Polly, then Beth Ann Pulaski and finally Donna Beaman. In the end, he'd resented their interference.

He never wanted to resent Edie.

Every time he looked at her, his heart melted a little. *Give it a try.*

But he was afraid. The little boy who'd had to fend for himself on the street was still buried inside him. The child who'd never experienced unconditional love and wasn't even sure such a thing existed.

He wasn't ready for this. Not while he was still playing Santa. Not while he was under strict orders not to reveal his identity to anyone.

Chief Timmons had no idea how grueling a punishment this assignment had become.

There had been no more thefts, and he'd managed to rule Joe and Kyle out as suspects. After talking with them, he'd discovered they both had air-tight alibis for each time something had turned up missing from the store.

Harry, however, was another story. As was Jules. Neither of them could adequately account for their whereabouts during several crucial incidents, and Harry's lie detector test had been inconclusive.

And there'd been that night when Sam had seen Harry in the mall parking lot. The same night Jules and Edie had broken into the store.

In the back of his mind, however, Sam was beginning to suspect someone else entirely. Someone previously beyond reproach. His suspicion had started that night in the department store. The night he'd heard someone in Trotter's office.

While he weighed the evidence and plotted his next course of action, Sam still worked side by side with Edie, playing Santa to her elf.

She kept her distance from him and she'd lost that familiar sparkle in her eyes. It hurt him to know he was the cause of her sadness.

But there was no way he could redeem himself. Not now. Not yet. Not until he knew for sure who was involved with the robberies. Once the case was solved, once she knew his true identity, maybe then they could start over.

TEARS WELLED IN Edie's eyes as she loaded film into the camera. It took her a minute to collect herself before she could look up and tell the next mother in line to put her child on Santa's lap.

She was tired of the silence between her and Sam. Ever since that night at his house things had been strained. He barely spoke more than he had to throughout the course of the day, and he spent a lot of time away from the sleigh. She no longer believed he was slipping off in search of booze or pills, but she couldn't help wondering where he went.

She glanced at Sam, but he avoided her gaze as he had all day long.

Now, she wished she had not pleaded with Dr. Braddick to let her do a case study on him. She was involved. She was hooked, addicted, enslaved by his kisses, desperate for more.

So what if he was working out his community service obligation as a store Santa? So what if he carried a concealed weapon in his boot? Obviously the stolen car incident had been a fluke, a one-time thing. And as far as her suspicions about his being involved with the store thefts—ludicrous! But it was almost Christmas and if she didn't do something soon, she'd probably never see him again.

Sam wasn't a thief. She'd bet her life on it.

That left her with one course of action. She'd tell him how foolish she'd been. How she'd been spying on him for her dissertation. She'd come clean. Hopefully, he wouldn't be too angry with her. Hopefully, this wouldn't get in the way of their budding relationship.

Tonight. She'd tell him tonight.

And let the chips fall where they may.

"MAYBE WE COULD grab a cup of coffee, Sam. I really need to talk to you," Edie said when the operator announced over the PA system that the store was closing in ten minutes.

"Uh, I have business with Mr. Trotter," he said.
"I'll catch you later."

Her face fell, and he knew he'd hurt her yet again.
Damn. This wasn't what he wanted. Not at all.

Edie gave a brave little shrug to show she didn't
care but the wounded expression in her eyes branded
him with guilt. "Sure. Later." Then quickly, before
he could say something to smooth things over, she
scurried away.

A notebook fell from her pocket.

"Wait," he called to her but apparently, she didn't
hear him for she just kept walking. Sam bent to re-
trieve the notebook.

He never meant to read it, but it lay open on the
floor and when he looked down, his name leapt out
at him.

Case Study—Sam Stevenson
Observation—December 23

He is not a bad boy at all. It's just a persona he
hides behind to protect himself. He is good and
kind and caring. He is tender and just and con-
cerned about the feelings of others. This observer
is certain he is not involved in the recent thefts
at Carmichael's Department Store. Problem—
Due to inappropriate behavior on the part of this
observer, the case study has been compromised.
Dissertation subject will have to be changed. Approval pending Dr. Braddick.

Sam's hands felt at once fiery hot and icy cold. He flipped the pages, started at the beginning and read how Edie had followed him, studied him.

Betrayed him.

He was her dissertation project.

Hard, bitter anger rose inside him. Edie was no different from Aunt Polly or Beth Ann Pulaski or Donna Beaman. He was nothing to her but a psychological endeavor.

And to think he'd thought he was falling in love with her!

Anger, hurt and resignation all ran through him. He tucked her notebook in his pocket. Well, that would teach him to care about someone. Sam plunked down in the sleigh, too stunned to move.

Then, from the corner of his eye, something caught his attention.

Freddie the Fish.

In the luggage aisle. The same place he'd been the first time Sam had kissed Edie.

Freddie was pushing past shoppers, his gaze scanning the room. Then from a side door Mr. Trotter appeared and motioned Freddie over. They talked together for a moment, heads bent, then Freddie followed Trotter back through the closed door that led to the warehouse.

Sam narrowed his eyes, and ducked down behind the sleigh. His instincts told him something was up.

What was Freddie the Fish doing with Trotter? The

suspicions he'd been entertaining for some time now expanded.

He climbed down from the dais and stalked through the crowd.

Children called to him. Shoppers waved as they lined up at the checkout stands. Sam forced a smile and walked faster. A few beard hairs flew into his mouth. His artificial belly shifted, throwing him off balance. Sam waddled to the door Trotter and Freddie had disappeared through. He lay his ear against the door and listened.

Nothing.

Taking a deep breath, he pried the door open and stepped through.

Except for the usual boxes of merchandise, this section of the storeroom was empty.

He cocked his head and listened intently.

No voices.

He squeezed past the boxes, turned a corner. His boots echoed in the hollow stillness.

They had disappeared awfully fast.

He kept walking.

Trotter and Freddie could have gone down any corridor; disappeared behind any door.

Damn.

Frustrated, he stopped, sank his hands on his hips and turned around.

He was in the main part of the warehouse now. The loading dock was a hundred yards to his left. It was after closing time and the place was deserted.

Sam scratched his head and leaned against a packing crate labeled Waste Materials.

What was happening to him? He was losing his edge. So what if Trotter was talking to Freddie? They could be related. Just because Trotter was consorting with a known thief that didn't mean the man was crooked.

He was letting Edie get to him. She was blowing his mind, messing with his head. She and her case study.

Sam kicked the crate.

The wood cracked, tearing the plastic wrapping beneath.

And revealing a box of brand-new radios that didn't look anything like waste materials.

WHERE WAS SAM GOING?

Edie had come back to the sleigh to look for her notebook and caught sight of Sam in his Santa suit as he disappeared through the door into the storeroom.

Because of the thefts, Trotter had warned all unauthorized personnel to stay out of the warehouse. Sam was violating store policy.

Why?

She no longer thought he was involved in the robberies but she wanted to get him alone and this was a good opportunity.

Yes. She had to speak to Sam. She couldn't stand not knowing how he felt about their relationship, about her. Especially since she'd decided she had to abandon her dissertation. Despite her best intentions, she'd fallen in love with him. She could not objectively do a case study on him. Dr. Braddick had been right.

Trotter or no Trotter, she was going after Sam.

Taking a deep breath to fortify herself for whatever might happen, she slipped through the empty store as "Blue Christmas" played on the stereo system.

"Sam," she called timidly, stepping around a stack of boxes.

Nothing. No one.

Hmm. She had seen him come in here. Couldn't mistake that Santa suit.

Nor the gorgeous man wearing it.

She trudged through the warehouse, alternately calling out his name, then stopping to scan the area for him.

A few minutes later, she heard a noise and turned the corner into the main warehouse.

And saw Sam digging in a large crate marked Waste Materials.

Except it wasn't waste materials in the box but electronic equipment. Radios, DVD players and computer components lay on the ground around him.

Edie looked at the merchandise and gulped.

Oh, Lord, don't let it be true after all!

"Sam," she said sharply, "what are you doing?"

"EDIE!" He felt his face flush a deep crimson beneath his white beard. "I—I—this isn't what you think."

"Are you trying to tell me you weren't stealing this equipment?" She waved a hand at the crate. The disappointment in her eyes was more than Sam could bear.

"You don't understand."

"Oh," she said. "I understand too well."

He ached to tell her that he wasn't a thief. But he couldn't blow his cover. Not now. Not when he was so close to finding out who had placed the items in the crate. And not when her own life could be at risk if she knew the truth.

He had only one choice. He had to lie to her.

Sam hung his head. "All right. You caught me. I'm the one who's been stealing from Carmichael's."

Her cry of dismay clawed him straight down to the bone. "Oh, Sam! How could you?"

He thought of her notebook in his pocket, pulled it out and handed it to her. "Seems you're not above a little deception yourself, Edie."

She stared at the notebook. "You read it?"

He nodded.

"I can explain."

He raised a hand. "Don't bother. Seems you were right about me from the first. I am a bad boy. Rotten to the core."

"No," she whispered. "Even after all this I can't believe that about you."

"Believe it," he said even though it killed him to utter those words. "Just as I have to deal with the fact that I was nothing more to you than a research project.''

''Sam, that's not true. Be fair.''

''You be fair, Edie. You followed me, used me, spied on me. What am I supposed to think?''

Her bottom lip trembled.

Ah, damn.

''You've got to turn yourself in to Mr. Trotter, Sam. It's the only way to make this right.''

''I can't.''

''Yes, you can. I'll go with you. I'll stand beside you. We'll get through this.''

''We?''

''Yes. Together. That is if you want me to help you.''

He shook his head. ''Can't resist meddling, can you sweetheart?''

''I'm not meddling.''

''You're so damned sexy when you're righteous.'' He took a step toward her. Her hands trembled slightly but she held her ground.

''Wh-what are you doing?'' she demanded.

''This.'' He had to test the depth of her feelings for him. Did she love him as a man? Or was he simply a project for her? Someone to reform. He needed an answer.

He took her in his arms and kissed her. He had to have one more taste of those irresistible lips before she disappeared from his life forever. Had to inhale her scent one last time. Had to feel the soft crush of her breasts against his chest.

And she didn't resist. She went limp in his arms for a moment, and then she flung her arms around his neck and kissed him back.

I'M HELPLESSLY HOOKED.

For the first time in her life, she understood the meaning of addiction. Edie felt crazed with emotion and wildly out of control.

She was addicted to his touch, his smile, his easy drawl. She needed him as desperately as flowers needed sun and rain and carbon dioxide.

Surely this relationship couldn't be healthy. She was falling for a criminal. Yet how could loving him be so wrong when it felt so perfect?

His kiss took her down, down, down in the torment of exquisite pleasure. He had no right to make her feel so good.

The sound of approaching voices killed the kiss. Sam pulled back.

"Someone's coming," she said. "You're going to have to give—"

Before she could say the words Sam clamped a hand over her mouth. "Shh, don't utter a sound."

Oh my gosh. Her breath rattled in her lungs like a loose shutter in the wind.

He grasped her around the waist and dragged her behind a ceiling-high shelf. He crouched low, taking her with him and shielding her head with his body.

Sam, don't do this, she mentally begged him and tried to squirm from his grip.

He held her firm, pressed his lips next to her ear. "Please, Edie," he whispered. "Don't fight me. Please, please just trust me."

Trust.

How could she trust a thief?

But oh, how she wanted to believe in him.

She'd counseled so many women who had done foolish things for the love of a man. Edie had sat in her psychologist's chair, passing judgment on people, offering her opinion on something when she'd had no real idea what she was talking about.

Now, she knew the power of love. At this moment, she could have forgiven Sam anything. Like a mother for her child, she loved him unconditionally. He didn't have to be a model citizen to earn her trust.

The voices grew louder. Two men were in the warehouse with them. Edie, who'd had her eyes tightly clenched, opened them and peered through a small hole in the boxes around them. She saw trousered legs and shoes.

She recognized one of the voices. Trotter.

Sam moved, letting her go and duck walking to the end of the shelf. In his hand he held the gun she'd seen the night they picked up the mannequin and he sang her his song.

The sight of the gun horrified her. What should she do?

"Someone's been in the crate!" the second man exclaimed.

Trotter cursed. "Get it loaded. Quickly. The truck is here."

Edie frowned. What did this mean?

Sam motioned for her to stay down.

"I told you the cops had someone undercover in the store."

"Shut up," Trotter said. "This is the last shipment. We won't be caught. I've planted some of the merchandise in the lockers of those men Carmichael made me hire from the halfway house."

Mr. Trotter was behind the thefts?

Dumbfounded, Edie's mouth dropped open. Well, if Trotter and his accomplice were the ones who'd been stealing from Carmichael's, who then was Sam?

The loading dock doors rolled up. Edie peeked around Sam's shoulder to see a large Carmichael's delivery truck backed against the platform.

"What's going on?" she whispered.

"Shh. Stay still."

But the more Edie thought about it, the madder she became. Trotter had stolen from the store, and now he was trying to blame it on Kyle, Harry and Joe.

Red-hot anger shot through her and before she had time to consider her actions, habit took over. She was not the type to let an injustice go unpunished.

Edie rose to her feet and marched forward. Sam grabbed for her ankle but missed. She rushed Trotter who was standing on the loading dock. He looked very startled to see her.

"Miss Preston," he exclaimed.

"You—you—creep! How dare you blame innocent people? How dare you steal from the store? This is inexcusable." Edie shook a finger at him.

Trotter's mouth dropped open, but only for a second. His eyes narrowed. He lunged for her and grabbed Edie by the hand.

"You're going to regret that speech, my dear," he said and pressed the cold, rude nose of a pistol flush against her temple. "Now, get into the back of the truck."

11
———————

DAMN HER SWEET, wonderful, impulsive hide.

He'd wanted to follow Trotter and Freddie, see where they were taking the stolen goods to fence. Now, his cover was about to be blown. They had his woman, and he would die before he let them leave the premises with her.

But Trotter had a gun pressed to her head.

Sam's gut roiled.

He stood, moved past the shelf and around the boxes. He raised his gun in both hands. "Police. Let her go, Trotter. It's not worth dying over."

"Police?" Edie's words echoed in the building. "You're a cop?"

Sam's eyes met hers. And darn if she didn't grin as big as a kid in a cotton-candy factory.

Trotter swung his gaze to Sam and cursed vehemently. Freddie the Fish was still tossing electronic equipment into the wooden crate. He stopped what he was doing and blinked. "Santa?"

"Sorry, Freddie, I'm afraid a sack of coal is all you're going to find in your stocking this Christmas. Get your hands over your head."

Sam turned the gun on Freddie. The man kept staring at him as if he couldn't believe he was being arrested by Santa Claus. Sam stepped over, relieved him of his gun and ordered him onto the ground. He cuffed Freddie, then trained his duty weapon on Trotter.

Trotter remained at the loading dock entrance, Edie clutched in his arms.

But the woman didn't have the presence of mind to be afraid. She kept haranguing him with words. Sam almost smiled.

"You should be ashamed of yourself," she lectured. "Didn't your mother teach you that it's not nice to point?"

"My mother's dead," Trotter said.

"Oh, I'm sorry."

Trotter shrugged. "That's life."

"Well, stop and think a moment. What will your wife say?"

"She left me. Ran off with an insurance executive. I didn't make enough money to please her," Trotter responded bitterly.

Sam watched Edie's face. He could see her mental cogs whirling. What was she up to?

"A man of your standing." Edie shook her head as if she didn't have a pistol against her temple. "Why would you do this?"

From his position on the ground, Freddie the Fish snorted. "He doesn't make enough to pay off his gambling debts. He's into my boss to the tune of two-hundred grand.''

''For shame!'' Edie scolded and Sam prayed Trotter wouldn't blow her away just to shut her up. ''And to think I had so much respect for you.''

Trotter blinked. ''You did?''

''Yes, but that was before I found out about this. How on earth do you expect to earn back my trust?''

The girl was nutty as a Christmas fruitcake, Sam concluded. He'd suspected this about her the moment they'd met when she'd tried to block him from stripping out of his flea-bitten Santa suit. Lucky for her, he was very fond of fruitcake.

Most women in the same predicament would sob or faint or freeze. Any of those responses would have been normal reactions.

But Edie Preston certainly was not normal.

Not by a long shot.

Her unconventional approach was one of the things he liked most about her.

''Well?'' Edie demanded. ''How do you expect to redeem your reputation?''

Trotter seemed confused. Sam used the opportunity to creep closer.

''What do you mean?'' Trotter asked, sweat beads popping out on his broad forehead. ''There's nothing to redeem. I'm going to kill you and Santa, then I'm going to load those electronics onto this truck and drive away.''

''Hey,'' Freddie protested. ''What about me?''

"You've set me up with the fence. You've served your purpose," Trotter said. "Maybe I'll shoot you, too. Place the gun in your hand. Make it look like you murdered them, then shot yourself out of remorse." Trotter paused to consider his new scenario. "Yes. It just might work. After all, as the girl said, I do have a reputation. Who would believe I was robbing the store?"

"It's not going to happen, Trotter. Put down the gun and let Edie go," Sam said tightly.

"You're in no position to be issuing orders, Stevenson."

Sam stared at Edie, peered deeply into her eyes. Silently, he sent her a message and prayed mental telepathy really worked. *Duck, run, move your head, anything to give me a clear shot at him.*

She didn't seem the least bit scared. Imperceptibly, she nodded. Had she understood what he wanted?

"This has gone on long enough, Mr. Trotter." Her voice was firm.

Then with a quick one-two action, she came down hard on his instep with her heel and drove her elbow backward into his gut.

"Ooph." Trotter's face darkened and he loosened his grip on her.

Run Edie, run.

But instead of moving out of the way, Edie turned inward, grasped Trotter's gun-toting wrist and bit him.

"Yow!" he yelped.

His gun clattered to the cement.

"Serves you right," Freddie the Fish mumbled from his low-level vantage point.

Sam didn't waste a second. He covered the ground between him and Trotter in two long-legged strides. He took the man by the collar and held on for dear life, his duty weapon pushed against Trotter's cheek. Let him have a dose of what he'd just dished out to Edie.

Pride for her welled inside him. "Are you all right?" he asked.

"Yeah!" She feigned boxing moves at Trotter, hopping from one foot to the other. Jab, jab, uppercut. "That'll teach you to mess with Santa Claus, you big bully."

The woman was too much. Sam grinned. "You made a mistake when you took this one as hostage, Trotter."

"Tell me about it." Trotter glowered. "I should have fired you both when I had the chance."

"Edie," Sam commanded. "Get the cell phone out of my hip pocket. Dial 911. Get them to patch you through to Chief Alfred Timmons. Tell him that Santa's got a surprise package waiting for him in Carmichael's warehouse."

SAM WAS A COP, Sam was a cop. Edie mentally chanted, grinning. She should have known her instincts about him hadn't led her astray. She hadn't made a mistake by falling in love with him.

She'd been waiting on a bench in the busy police station for over three hours. She'd already given her statement to one of the officers who'd arrived to help Sam cart off Trotter and his unhappy accomplice.

Now, she was waiting for Sam to wrap up the details of the arrest. They had a lot to discuss.

Like what the future might hold.

An eager excitement fizzed inside her and Edie struggled to quell her nervousness.

When Sam finally emerged from behind closed doors minus the Santa suit, his dark hair combed back off his head, a gun holster at his hip, a badge pinned on his chest, Edie's heart tripped.

He was so handsome. So forceful. So manly. He was chatting to another officer and he hadn't seen her yet. She gulped and held her breath.

Her nervousness transformed into something much more palpable.

Fear.

A million what-ifs rose to her mind. What if he didn't want her? What if she had somehow screwed things up between them?

She pushed aside her fears. Edie wasn't one to sit and wonder. For better or worse, she was the type to grab the bull by the horns and demand answers.

He finished his conversation and started across the room. Phones rang, computer keyboards clacked, voices hummed but Edie could scarcely hear anything over the steady pounding of her heart.

Rising to her feet, she moved toward him.

"Sam."

"Edie." He stopped.

Anxiously she studied his face, searching for a sign.

"You're still here."

"Yes."

"I thought you'd be long gone." He smiled faintly. A smile was a good thing. Yes?

"I wanted to talk to you."

"That's good. I needed to talk to you too."

"You do?"

His features turned serious. "Do you have any idea how foolhardy you acted today?" He shook his head. "I can't believe you simply charged over to Trotter and started lecturing him."

"He had it coming." She notched her chin upward.

"Edie, he is a dangerous man, he had a gun. Didn't you think about that?"

"I could only think about one thing," she said.

"And what was that?"

"How he was trying to frame the other guys. Blame them for his wrongdoings. He had to be held accountable. I couldn't sit by and do nothing."

"Fools rush in," Sam muttered and shook his head.

Her heart knocked painfully against her chest. He thought she was a fool.

"Did you learn anything from this?" he asked.

"What do you mean?"

"About rushing into situations without enough information."

"Now that you mention it," she admitted. "I was pretty scared."

A smiled crooked one corner of his mouth. "I never would have guessed. You were cucumber cool. And you really threw Trotter off guard. When we were interrogating him, he kept saying 'that girl wouldn't stop lecturing me.'"

"Really?"

"You've got high expectations of people, Edie Preston."

She couldn't mistake the twinkle in his eye. That was a good sign.

Right?

"Do you need a ride home?" He angled his head.

"I thought you'd never ask."

"This way." He placed a hand to the small of her back and guided her to the door and into the night.

Edie gnawed on her bottom lip, wished desperately she'd had her makeup kit with her so she could freshen up. Unfortunately, she was also in her elf suit with the darned jangling jingle bells.

Please, she thought, *just let me survive the drive home. Let me find the right words to tell him how I feel about him.*

When they reached the parking lot, he stopped beside his car and took her hand.

"Listen, Edie, I want you to know that I've had a great time these past five weeks playing Santa with you."

Oh, no. Here it comes. You're a great girl but...

"Me, too," she whispered, her gaze scanning his face, searching for answers.

"You're a great girl."

Her stomach roiled. Her hands trembled. Tears gathered behind her eyelids.

So much for taking a walk on the wild side.

"You're a wonderful guy." She blinked. Willed away the tears.

"I know I'm not good enough for you. I grew up the hard way, on the streets. I spent my youth rebelling against authority. If it hadn't been for my Aunt Polly..." He shook his head. "But I digress. I'm a cop. I see the dark-and-dirty side of life. You're an optimist. You're clean and pure and innocent. I'm afraid..." He stopped.

"Afraid of what?" she urged.

He took a deep breath. Were those tears glistening in his eyes? Her heart stuttered.

"If we start dating that I'll ruin what I love most about you."

What he loved most about her? Her pulse quickened.

"Your inherent belief in the goodness of your fellow man."

A lock of hair had fallen across his forehead. She raised on tiptoes, patted the strand back into place.

"Shh," she said. "Don't be silly. We're perfect together. I need your cold-eyed realism just as much as you need my cockeyed optimism. You've taught me so much about life, Sam Stevenson, in such a short time.''

''Same here.'' His voice was gruff.

''For so many years I've been like everyone's kid sister. Guys don't make passes at me. Construction workers don't whistle at me on the street. I'm the good girl. But you make me feel like a real woman. Alive, sexy, sexual. You've given me the courage to take risks, to really experience life. I can't tell you how good that feels.''

''Really?''

She nodded.

He actually blushed. Big, tough cop didn't know how to take a compliment. ''Well, you make me feel pretty sexy, too. The last thing I ever expected was to fall in love with you.''

Emotions knotted in her throat. ''You're in love with me?''

''Hell, yes,'' he said gruffly. ''Why do you think I was trying to break things off with you?''

''Is that what you usually do when you're in love? Run away?''

''I'm scared I can't live up to your expectations. I was worried you'd pass judgement on me. That I wouldn't measure up to your expectations. Aunt Polly wanted so much from me. So did my last girlfriend. I can't offer you anything more than what you see right now, Edie. Take me as I am. For better or worse.'' He held his arms wide, exposing himself to her.

Instinctively, she knew this was a very difficult thing for him to do—lay himself bare.

"And if I say yes?"

"Then I'm taking you back to my place."

"Yes," she said. "Yes, yes, a thousand times yes."

Embracing the exhilarating insanity of the moment, Edie climbed into the Corvette beside him and snapped her seat belt into place. He drove through the light traffic to his quaint house in his eclectic neighborhood.

I'd love living here, she realized, in this melting pot of cultures.

Sam pulled into the driveway and leapt from the car, hustling around to the passenger side to help her out.

He ushered her up the steps and across the threshold, both their breaths coming in sharp, hurried gasps. He positioned her on the couch, then turned on the stereo.

"Walking in a Winter Wonderland," issued forth.

He joined her on the couch and pulled her into his lap. "Christmas will always be our special time," he whispered, his warm breath feathering the hairs back from her ears.

"We won't be able to hear a Christmas song without thinking back on this moment," he continued.

"Or see a sprig of mistletoe without remembering the first time you kissed me."

"You mean like this?" Sam kissed her softly, gently, repeatedly.

"More like this," Edie said, introducing her tongue into the mix.

"Whew." He pulled back a few minutes later.

"When you take a walk on the wild side, you really take a walk on the wild side."

"I learned from the best." She grinned.

"I love the way you smile," he said.

"I love the way you smell." She buried her nose against his neck. "Like pine cones and peppermint and gingerbread."

He caught her chin in his palm, turned her face to meet his eyes. "And I love you, Edie Preston, with all my heart and soul."

"I love you, too, Sam," she whispered. "More than you'll ever know."

He rose to his feet, Edie clutched firmly in his arms. Her giggle echoed in the room. "Where are we going?" she demanded.

"To the bedroom."

"Ah."

"Got a problem with that?"

"No. Not at all. But I do have one request."

"And that is?"

"Do you still have the Santa suit?" she whispered. "Because I've always had this wild little fantasy..."

Modern Romance™
...seduction and
passion guaranteed

Tender Romance™
...love affairs that
last a lifetime

Sensual Romance™
...sassy, sexy and
seductive

Blaze.
...sultry days and
steamy nights

Medical Romance™
...medical drama on
the pulse

Historical Romance™
...rich, vivid and
passionate

27 new titles every month.

*With all kinds of Romance for
every kind of mood...*

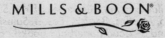

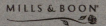

MILLS & BOON®

Tender Romance™

READER SERVICE™

The best romantic fiction direct to your door

Our guarantee to you...

The Reader Service involves you in no obligation to purchase, and is truly a service to you!

There are many extra benefits including a free monthly Newsletter with author interviews, book previews and much more.

Your books are sent direct to your door on 14 days no obligation home approval.

We offer huge discounts on selected books exclusively for subscribers.

Plus, we have a dedicated Customer Care team on hand to answer all your queries on
(UK) 020 8288 2888
(Ireland) 01 278 2062.

GEN/GU/1